MEMORIES OF THE FUTURE

GEORGE IVANOFF

CANDY JAR BOOKS · CARDIFF
2022

Range Editor: Shaun Russell
Cover: Steve Beckett
Editorial: Will Rees & Keren Williams
Continuity Editor: Andy Frankham-Allen

ISBN: 978-1-915439-36-9

Printed and bound in the UK by
4edge, 22 Eldon Way, Hockley, Essex, SS5 4AD

Published by
Candy Jar Books
Mackintosh House
136 Newport Road, Cardiff, CF24 1DJ
www.candyjarbooks.co.uk

For all those involved with Aussiecon Two, organisers and attendees. Held in 1985, it was the first convention I ever attended, and after all these years I still have such fond memories of it.

– PROLOGUE –

REMEMBER

'What sort of story would you like today, Lucyloo?'

'Tell me about the units.' Lucy was literally quivering with anticipation as she sat on her grandad's knee.

'The units?' There was a knowing, mischievous gleam in the old man's eyes that didn't match the puzzlement in his voice.

'Oh, you know, Grandad... the soldier men.'

'Ah, of course. You mean UNIT. The United Nations Intelligence Taskforce.'

'That's right, the soldier men who fought the aliens.'

Grandad chuckled. 'Yes, UNIT certainly did fight some pretty nasty alien types. But they weren't all men, you know. There were women as well. We had a very clever scientist working with us for a while and she was a woman.' He nodded at his granddaughter and tapped the end of her nose with his shaky finger. 'And there was even a woman in charge of UNIT for a while.'

'I thought you were the soldier boss?' said Lucy, concerned that someone other than her grandfather could possibly be in command.

'Well, yes, I suppose I was. For a time anyway. But things changed. And I retired.' He paused for a moment, his eyes getting that faraway, unfocused look they acquired when he became lost in his memories. Lucy waited patiently until he again looked down at her, his eyes coming back to the present, his smile creasing his face, just for her. 'Anyway, have I ever told you about the time UNIT faced…?'

Lucy loved these stories so much. And she loved spending time with her grandfather. As she grew up, these precious moments would become some of her most cherished memories…

The sort of memories that stayed with you forever.

The sort of memories that would never fade.

LUCY

– CHAPTER ONE –

AUSTRALIA?

AUSTRALIA? Lucy stared at the stamps on the letter as she sat down on the end of her bed in Ogmore-by-Sea, Wales. There was no return address, so they were the only clue she had as to where the letter had come from. But she didn't know anyone in Australia. Did she?

And it felt like there was something firm in there – more than just a letter.

Lucy sniffed. There was a floral smell in her room. Quite pleasant really. Maybe her mum had brought flowers into her room. She gazed around. No flowers. But her wardrobe door wasn't shut properly. Had her mum been in her things? She'd ask her later.

She looked back down at the envelope and peeled up the edge of the seal, slipping her pinkie inside, using it to tear open the envelope. She pulled out a neatly folded piece of paper. As she unfolded it, something fell out. Lucy turned the paper over in her hands, puzzled that it was blank, then glanced down at the floor. A dog-eared, blurry old Polaroid photo lay on the carpet. *Who takes Polaroids anymore?* she thought. Using your phone is way more instant.

As she leaned down to pick up the photo, the ring that hung on a chain around her neck fell forward into her line of sight. Had it just been glowing?

This was a very special ring, given to her by Dame Anne, an old friend of her grandfather. It was a ring that enabled her to travel through time. Was it suggesting a trip now? She undid the chain and slipped the ring onto her finger. But nothing happened.

She sighed and reached down again for the photo.

But then her vision wavered. Darkness crept in from the edges as she lost focus.

The ring on her finger felt warm. It pulsed, almost as if it were alive.

She inhaled sharply. There was that smell again.

Her head spun.

The photo slipped from her fingers.

And the blackness closed in.

MATTY

– CHAPTER TWO –

THE MYSTERIOUS GIRL WHO APPEARED OUT OF NOWHERE

Invading aliens or time travel? It was a difficult decision but it had to be made

Given his pocket-money situation, Matty could only afford to buy one new book every three weeks or so, depending on his other spending. Plus, he'd also been saving for the upcoming convention. His school library filled in the time between new books, but it rarely had the latest science fiction novels he so craved.

Matty sat down on the bottom of the stairs and opened the first book. *I'll just read the first chapter of each,* he thought. *That will help me decide which one to spend my money on.*

'See ya Friday for the con,' called Fred, as he headed out of the shop.

Matty waved goodbye to his best friend and settled in to read.

A few minutes later, he was startled out of the depths of space by the sounds of movement from above. A shuffle, followed by a thump and then a groan. Matty looked over his shoulder and up the stairs. There shouldn't have been anyone on the first floor. He'd been the last one to leave the meeting today, tidying up the books and magazines before coming down into the shop on the ground floor. The owner of the shop, Space/Time Books, allowed him and his group of high school sci-fi enthusiasts to use the room above once a week, to hold their meetings after school. It made good business sense, as all those teenagers tended to then spend their pocket money in store.

Matty put the book down on the bottom step and got to his feet. It was probably just his imagination, he told himself. But there was a difference between what he told himself and what he actually believed. Slowly, carefully, one tentative step at a time, he ascended.

His jaw dropped as he entered the room – dropped and hung open. There was a girl lying on the floor. Dressed in blue jeans, a black t-shirt and red hoodie, with white runners, she was sprawled out on the scuffed wooden boards.

She was either unconscious or dead. Either way,

Matty thought she was rather good looking. She had warm brown skin and an explosion of unruly dark curls that revealed a pretty face. He hoped she wasn't dead. He really wanted to ask her for her name.

But how had she come to be here? The only way into this room was up the stairs and she would have had to pass right by him. The window was not an option as it had been painted shut years ago. Had she materialised out of nowhere? He found himself getting excited by that thought. Maybe she had fallen through a dimensional wormhole? Been deposited by a transporter beam from an alien spaceship in orbit? Or even better, thrown through a space/time vortex? A space/time vortex in Space/Time Books. What a ridiculously cool idea! On the other hand, it might be something far more ordinary and boring. Maybe she had simply snuck past him as he deliberated over books?

She groaned and stirred.

Great, thought Matty, *she isn't dead.*

As her eyes fluttered open, he finally closed his mouth.

'What happened?' mumbled the girl, as she struggled into a sitting position. She saw Matty and stared at him for a few seconds. Then her eyes darted about, checking out the room with its battered bookshelves and fold out chairs. She paused and

Matty followed her gaze to the far wall covered in Polaroid photographs. It was Marvin's hobby, taking photos of famous (and not-so-famous) people who visited his shop. The celebrity photos were all downstairs behind the counter, while the rest got stuck up here.

The girl's attention snapped back to Matty and she jumped to her feet. She was about his height, which wasn't very tall at all.

'Who are you?' she demanded. 'Where am I? What am I doing here?'

'Matthew Franklin,' said Matty. 'But most people just call me Matty. And this is Space/Time Books. As for what you're doing here... not a clue!' He paused and smiled at her. 'So, what's your name?'

'Good question,' she responded. 'It's... um... well...' Her brow crinkled in concentration. 'It's a long name.'

Matty nodded encouragingly, not wanting this odd girl to know just how weird he thought she was.

'Lucy.' She blurted it out triumphantly, then frowned. 'I think.'

'Sounds short to me.' The corner of Matty's mouth quirked into a half-smile.

'Yes...' The mysterious girl, who might be named Lucy, frowned. 'There's more to it, I'm sure. I... I just... can't remember.'

'I don't suppose you know how you got in here?'

asked Matty.

Lucy shook her head.

'Do you remember anything at all? Where you live? Age? Favourite food?'

'Um, I'm fourteen. I like pasta and chocolate.' She shrugged. 'And that's about it.'

'Everyone likes chocolate.' Matty walked across the room to stand awkwardly beside her. 'Hmmm, sound likes you've got amnesia.'

'Yeah. I guess.'

Matty didn't think she sounded all that convinced.

'Okay.' Matty scratched an eyebrow thoughtfully. 'So, I'm going to throw some random questions at you. Just to test out what you remember. You okay with that?'

'I suppose so.'

'Cool!' Matty rubbed his hands together in anticipation. 'What year is it?'

'No idea.'

'What country are we in?'

'Don't know.'

'City?'

'Don't know that either.'

'Brothers or sisters?'

'Maybe.'

'Parents?'

'Yes!' Lucy almost shouted. 'I've got parents. I'm

sure of that.'

'Great! Names?'

'Ahhh....'

'Grandparents?'

'I've got a grandad,' said Lucy with certainty. 'And he's important.'

Beep! Beep! Beep!

'What's that?' demanded Lucy, head whirling from side to side. She looked like she was ready to bolt.

'Calm down. Just the alarm on my digital watch,' said Matty. 'Got it for my fifteenth birthday. I set alarms to remind me of stuff, like making sure I don't spend too much time browsing books and forget to catch the train.'

'Train?' asked Lucy.

'Train,' said Matty slowly. 'It's a long vehicle that travels upon rails and—'

'Oh, I know what a train is,' huffed Lucy.

'Cool.'

'Where are you taking this train?'

'Home.'

'And where's that?'

'Mentone,' said Matty. Lucy stared blankly at him, so he elaborated. 'It's a suburb of Melbourne. About halfway between the city and Frankston.'

'Melbourne,' whispered Lucy. 'Melbourne. That's... that's in Australia.'

'Yes!' Matty grinned. 'The city of Melbourne. In the state of Victoria. In the country of Australia. In the southern hemisphere of the planet Earth. Within the solar sys—'

'Do you always go on like that?' interrupted Lucy.

'Like what?' Matty put on a mock-pouty face.

'Never mind.'

'I'm guessing you're not from around here,' continued Matty.

'Why do you say that?'

'Your accent. Duh!' He made a silly face at her. 'You sound like a Pom.'

'I beg your pardon?' Now it was Lucy's turn to look pouty.

'A Brit,' Matty corrected himself. 'Sorry.'

'You're forgiven.' She smiled. Matty decided that he liked her smile. It was friendly and genuine.

'Anyway, knowing that Melbourne is in Australia is good. This is progress. I reckon you'll get your memory back. It's just a matter of time.' His smile turned into a thoughtful expression. 'But what'll we do with you in the meantime?'

'Huh?'

'Well, you can't stay here.' Matty waved his arms around, almost knocking into Lucy. 'This is a bookshop and it'll be closing soon.'

'Oh.'

Matty had the overwhelming urge to keep her

with him. Her appearance out of nowhere was a mystery – like something from a film – and his mind kept coming back to potential sci-fi explanations. He wanted to solve this mystery. To find out if she really had materialised in a blaze of otherworldliness. Of course, he knew that the logical thing to do, the sensible thing, would be to go to the police. They had the best chance of finding out who she really was. They could get a doctor to check her out and perhaps do something about the amnesia. But…

'I suppose you could come home with me,' suggested Matty.

'Oi! Where do youse think you're goin'?'

Matty and Lucy froze at the door, then slowly turned to face the man behind the counter.

'I ain't got a photo of your girlfriend,' he said, fishing a battered old Polaroid camera out from under the cash register.

'What? No!' Matty felt his face flush with heat. 'She's not my… she's just… I mean… we only just met.'

'G'day, not-Matty's-girlfriend,' said the man, putting down the camera and extending a hand towards Lucy. 'My name's Marvin. And I'm the proprietor of this 'ere establishment of the imagination.'

Matty wondered why there was never a lighting strike, or earthquake or alien invasion around when you really needed something to distract the attention of a well-meaning but thoroughly embarrassing adult. Mind you, as far as adults went, Marvin was kind of okay. Tall and slightly chubby, his head was bald, but he had really thick ginger eyebrows and a goatee beard. Matty always thought that he'd make a good Bond villain.

On the wall behind the counter were all his good Polaroids. Mostly sci-fi and fantasy authors holding copies of their own books while standing in his store. There were Australian authors like Lee Harding and Terry Dowling, as well as internationally famous ones like Ursula K Le Guin and Terrance Dicks.

Lucy took his hand and shook it, but when she tried to let go, Marvin clung on, staring at her hand, eyes wide.

'You're wearing a ring,' he said.

'Um, yes, I guess I am.' She managed to yank her hand back. 'Is that a problem?'

'No, it's just that...' He paused. 'It's a very unusual ring. That stone. Where d'ya get it?'

'Um,' Lucy looked blankly at Marvin. 'I don't know.'

'Ya don't know?'

'She's got amnesia,' Matty butted in. 'She can't remember anything.'

'Am-nes-i-a,' said Marvin, enunciating each syllable. 'So, she—'

Beep, beep, beep!

Saved by the bell. Well... the beep.

Matty pressed the button on the side of his watch to stop the sound. 'Sorry, Marvin, can't chat. Got to go or we'll miss the train. Then I'll be late. And then my parents will be mad at me.' He took hold of Lucy's arm and started to lead her out the door. 'And you don't want me to get into trouble.'

As the two of them headed up the narrow alleyway towards Bourke Street, Matty glanced back over his shoulder. Marvin was watching them, nose pressed up against the door, fogging up the glass.

LUCY

– CHAPTER THREE –

TRAIN TRIP

Clackety-clack! Clackety-clack! Clackety-clack! Lucy wondered why she was so calm. Surely she should be panicking? She still remembered how to talk, and she still knew some of the basics about herself, but she had forgotten so much. Who was she? Why was she here in Melbourne all on her own? And why wasn't she scared? Maybe she'd forgotten how to be scared?

Clackety-clack! Clackety-clack! Clackety-clack!

She realised that she was playing with the ring on her finger, slipping it on and off. It didn't fit very well. She wondered why she would be wearing an ill-fitting ring. Just one more thing she had no memory of. There was something about it. Something special. But she had no idea what.

Clackety-clack! Clackety-clack! Clackety-clack!

She looked up. The train had been really crowded when she and Matty had got on, full of kids in school uniform and grown-ups in business suits, but with each stop more of them disembarked. There was now only a smattering of people in their carriage, and they had their row to themselves.

Clackety-clack! Clackety-clack! Clackety-clack!

Lucy still couldn't get over how cheap the train ticket had seemed. But she couldn't figure out why she thought that, since she couldn't actually remember what she thought a train ticket should cost. It was very puzzling.

Clackety-clack! Clackety-clack! Clackety-clack!

Lucy tried to think over the sound of the train. Her mind was a whirl of thoughts and images that she just couldn't decipher. Things at the edge of her memory that she couldn't quite grasp. Faces just out of focus. Places just out of reach.

And a name she couldn't remember. A long name. Was it hers?

Clackety-clack! Clackety-clack! Clackety-clack!

Were trains usually this loud? She thought that they should be quieter. Smoother. But she couldn't produce a memory to back it up. She glanced over at Matty, awkwardly seated opposite her, and asked anyway.

'Why is this train so loud?'

'Is it?' The boy called Matty gave her a puzzled expression. 'It's quieter than the old Red Rattlers. They were a lot noisier. Hence the name. But there are no more of them around. They got rid of the last of them in '84 because they had asbestos in them. Pity. I kinda liked them. This is a Harris train, but everyone just calls them blue trains... 'cause, you know... they're blue.'

This boy talks a lot, thought Lucy. She momentarily wondered what a Red Rattler was, but her mind quickly fixed on something else Matty had said.

'84,' she repeated. '1984.'

'Yeah. Just like that famous book,' said Matty, slowly. 'It was last year. This year is 1985.'

'Is it?' Lucy frowned. Why did that seem so unbelievable?

'Yep. Today is Monday the twentieth of August 1985.'

Lucy stared at Matty. Dressed in a grey, nondescript school uniform, he was an odd looking boy, she thought. Hair that was so blond, it was almost white, which meant that his eyebrows and lashes seemed to disappear against his pale skin. His dark eyes, greeny-brown, contrasted sharply. He was about her height – short. And slight of build. Her overall impression of him was that he appeared delicate... fragile... frail almost.

What in the world was she doing, going home with him? This boy she had only just met. What if he was an axe-wielding serial killer? She had no reason to trust him and yet, strangely, she did.

She turned away the moment she realised that she had been staring, eyes now wandering around the carriage instead. The walls were a pale cream, broken up by occasional bits of graffiti, and the uncomfortable seats were covered in a stiff grey-patterned fabric. There were a couple of teenagers at the other end of the carriage, snogging, a businessman reading a newspaper and trying to ignore the teenagers, a few other nondescript people, and a woman seated in the row behind them. Lucy's attention focused on her. There was something not right. She was dressed in a steel-grey suit and was reading a book while wearing dark sunglasses. Lucy gazed out the window as suburban houses streaked by – it was overcast. She looked back at the woman, her white hair in a neat bob – pure, stark white rather than the white-blond of Matty's hair. Her face wasn't angled at the book. It was tilted towards them.

'Why is that woman watching us?' hissed Lucy.

Matty glanced over his shoulder. 'The woman with the book and glasses?' he asked, and then continued without waiting for an answer. 'She's not watching us. She's reading!'

'Her book is upside down,' Lucy pointed out.

Matty turned back and leaned over the seat, listening intently. He waved at the woman (who didn't react) then turned to face Lucy, smiling. 'She's snoring.'

'But she's still holding the book.' Lucy didn't want to let go of her suspicions. There was something not right about that woman.

'So she's got a good sleep-grip,' said Matty, with a grin.

The train stopped and it was time to get off. Matty led her onto the platform, a white sign with black lettering telling them they were at MENTONE STATION.

As they walked along the platform, the train went on its way. Lucy peered through the window as their carriage passed by, but the woman was gone.

MATTY

– CHAPTER FOUR –

HOME IS WHERE THE OVERGROWN YARD IS

'Here it is,' announced Matty, arms spread wide, face lit up with pride. 'Home sweet home!'

'Is this where you live?' asked Lucy.

Matty's face dropped. She didn't sound at all impressed, or even enthusiastic. 'Ah... yeah.'

She turned away from the green fence to look up and down the quiet suburban street. Matty followed her gaze. He supposed that his place was different from all the others, with their low brick fences or white pickets. They had an openness to them. Whereas his place, well, it gave off a don't-look-at-me vibe. He glanced back at the high, solid wooden fence that surrounded his house. Painted green, it blended in with the unruly camellias that exploded above it, effectively concealing the house. He briefly wondered why his parents had decided to do that, cut the house off from the rest of the street. And then he wondered why he had never wondered about it before.

He shook the thought away and turned back to the suburban vista. It was a mild winter's day and the streetlights were starting to flicker into life as the early twilight descended. There were some younger kids a few houses up, playing cricket out on the street. Mrs Purchess, the elderly lady who lived across the road, was out watering her garden (she *always* seemed to be out, watering her garden). She waved and he raised a tentative hand in response. She continued to watch him as she hosed her rose bushes.

Matty looked at Lucy and blushed. He was bringing a girl home with him. No wonder Mrs P was staring at him. He wondered at the sanity of what he was doing.

'Um, let's go.'

He led Lucy through the gate, closing it behind them, blocking off the view from prying eyes.

'Oh, wow!'

Lucy was staring around in wonderment. While the house was just an ordinary old weatherboard bungalow with peeling paint and sagging gutters, the garden was more unusual. Lush was a good word to describe it. Overgrown was another.

'This is...'

'Unkempt!' Matty finished for her.

'Awesome!' breathed Lucy.

'Really?' Matty loved the garden. He loved how many plants his parents managed to fit into their yard. Their house was set deep into the property, a result of subdivision decades earlier, and so they had little more than a paved veranda in the back, but a spacious area out front. He loved the variety of plants – everything from the camellias that stood by the front fence, to the towering gumtree in the corner, to the orange and lemon trees that obscured the front porch, and all the low growing shrubs and potted herbs. He loved the feeling of it all – how the vegetation seemed to create its own little ecosystem, a biome of calm away from the surrounding suburbia. It washed away any doubts he had about bringing Lucy home with him. 'Glad you like it.'

'How long have you lived here?' she asked.

'Oh... ah... like, forever. I think.' He certainly didn't remember having lived anywhere else. So he must have lived here his whole life. He realised that he'd never actually asked his parents if they'd ever lived anywhere else. Not that it mattered.

They stood in silence for few minutes, enjoying the serenity, until the distant sound of laughing children made Matty start.

'Um... we should get inside.'

*

As he gave Lucy a tour of his home, Matty again began to question the sanity of what he was doing, bringing a stranger – a girl – home with him. Now that she was here, what was he going to do with her? What would his parents say?

'And this is... um... well, it's my bedroom,' stumbled Matty, wondering why he was suddenly feeling so warm.

'Could use a tidy up,' said Lucy, peering through the doorway but not stepping in.

'Oh.' The heat drained from his face.

'Right,' said Lucy, turning to face him. 'Now what?'

'Um...'

'For someone who talks a lot, you're sometimes not very good with words.' Lucy put her hands on her hips. 'Now that I'm here, in your home, what do we do? How are we going to get my memory back?'

'Oh, yeah, your memory. I forgot.'

Lucy rolled her eyes. 'Tell me you're kidding.'

'Just a momentary lapse,' Matty assured her. 'We will work on restoring your memory. We need to prompt it. Remind it of what it's forgotten. We need...'

Matty heard the front door open and voices drifting down the corridor.

'My parents,' he whispered. 'Better that they

don't know you're here.' His eyes glazed over, as his brain quickly tried to assess the situation and how he should respond. 'Ah… you go into my room. Sorry about the mess. Try not to make any noise. I'll keep my parents busy and come back later. In the meantime, you can look around. Ah, like, not in my underwear draw or anywhere like that, though. And um, why don't you read something. It might help with your memory. Yeah. Look through my books and mags. Oh. Ah. But not the ones under my bed. Yeah. So. Okay.' He ushered her inside. 'See you.' And closed the door.

He leaned back against the door, closed his eyes, berated himself, took a deep breath, opened his eyes and headed off down the corridor in what he hoped was a casual and unworried way.

'Hey,' he said, coming into the kitchen where his parents were starting the dinner preparations.

'Hey yourself,' his mum responded, as she rummaged through the pantry.

'Have a good time with your sci-fi mates?' asked his dad, not even looking up from the chopping board.

'Um… yeah, I guess.'

They only just glanced at him, then continued with what they were doing.

Matty watched them, wondering what to do and say in order to sound normal and unconcerned. The two of them always tried to cook dinner together. Mum would plan. Dad would chop things. Then Mum would do the actual cooking part while Dad set the table. They reckoned that it brought them closer together. Dinner! That was it! He could ask them about dinner.

'Is it going to be a big meal?'

'That's an odd question,' said Mum, turning away from the pantry to raise an eyebrow at him.

'Is it? Oh. Sorry! It's just that I'm really hungry today. So, yeah. What is for dinner?'

'Spag Bol,' answered Dad.

'Cool! Okay then. I'll just go and hang out in my room until it's ready. Okay!'

'No-kay,' said Mum. 'Since you're so keen on dinner tonight, why don't you help out?'

'Oh… well…'

'Great,' said Dad. 'You can start by grating the cheese.' He chuckled to himself as he fetched the cheddar from the fridge. 'You're so great at grating.' And he burst into gales of laughter.

Matty groaned.

'You really do amuse yourself, don't you, dear,' said Mum.

Matty found that he couldn't escape. His parents kept him busy with food prep and idle chatter about things he couldn't keep his mind on. Something about homework and grades and whatever. He nodded and smiled frequently, without any idea what he was responding to, his mind completely occupied with the mysterious girl in his bedroom. His! Bedroom!

By the time dinner had been cooked and eaten, he had everything worked out.

'I'll clear the table,' he announced, jumping to his feet, as his parents stared in disbelief. 'And I might eat a little more. I'm still a bit hungry.'

'Sure.' Mum gave him a half-smile then widened her eyes at Dad, who shrugged in response.

Carrying the dishes to the kitchen, Matty stacked the dishwasher, gathered up a portion of the leftovers into a plastic bowl, before storing the rest in the fridge. Then he was off to his room.

'Brought you some dinner,' he said, slipping into his bedroom and closing the door behind him.

Lucy looked up from the book she was reading. She appeared to have made herself quite comfortable on his bed, books spread out around her. 'I'm going to take a wild stab in the dark and say that you're *really* into sci-fi.' She indicated all the collectable paraphernalia that littered the room.

'Well, we did meet in a science fiction bookshop.'

'True.' She closed the atlas she'd been perusing and tossed it onto the bed, swinging her legs around and sitting up. 'I've been going through your school books in the hopes of jogging my memory. I thought an atlas might help me remember where I'm from.'

'And has it?'

'Maybe. Not sure.' She frowned. 'The UK seems familiar. Possibly.'

'Well, it would explain your accent.'

'It's funny, I keep thinking that other bits of the atlas are wrong.'

'Like?'

'Oh, the USSR. And Kampuchea. Other stuff.' She shook her head as if to dismiss the thoughts. 'Anyway, what've you got for me?'

'Spaghetti Bolognaise.'

'Yum!'

Matty watched as the strange girl devoured the food like she hadn't eaten in forever. His gaze wandered and a smile played at the corners of his mouth. He really did like sci-fi. He guessed that to someone who didn't, his room might be considered a little weird. *The Millennium Falcon,* two tie fighters and the *Battlestar Galactica* hung from the ceiling on strings. There were lots of bookshelves full of science fiction books (and a bit of fantasy as well, 'cause everyone should read *The Lord of the Rings* at least once), with the remaining wall space plastered with movie posters – everything from *Star Wars* to *Supergirl*; from *2001: A Space Odyssey* to *Battle Beyond the Stars*. Somewhere in amongst all this was his bed, with an R2D2 bedspread, and a small desk at which he did his homework. His terrarium, like a mini-jungle encased in glass, sat on the desk. It was like having a little bit of the front yard with him in his room.

'Do I get the R2D2 bed?'

Matty's eyes snapped back to Lucy. She'd finished eating and was looking at him.

'R2D2? You know who he is?'

'Well, yeah. Doesn't everybody?'

'That's a memory! That's great. And R2D2 is a great character. And *Star Wars* is such a great film series. So you've got a great memory about a great character from a great film.'

'Yeah… although *The Phantom Menace* is a bit pants!' said Lucy. 'I saw it in 3D with—'

'But that's my bed,' said Matty, interrupting.

'So where do I sleep then? You're not going to hide me in the garage or something, are you?' said Lucy.

'No, of course not.' Matty had actually considered that option. His parents didn't own a car, so they never went into the garage. It would have been perfect. But it would also be cold and uncomfortable, he supposed. 'We've got a spare room. It's full of boxes and kind of a mess. Disaster area really. But there's an old mattress in there up against the wall behind all those boxes. So I could rearrange things and make a bit of room for you. And Mum and Dad hardly ever go in there, so it should be safe. Oh, and it's right next door to me.'

'Is this them?' Lucy picked up the framed photo of Matty and his parents that rested on the shelf beside his bed.

'Uh-huh.'

'When was this taken?'

'Oh... um... not sure.' Matty wracked his brain, but couldn't remember when the photo was from. Or where. It must have been fairly recent, because he wasn't any younger than he was now. And yet, he had this vague thought that it had always been there, sitting on the shelf beside his bed.

'They don't look much like you.' It was an off-handed comment, but it took Matty by surprise. 'You're blond, they're dark haired. They're both kind of solid and broad and you're... not.'

Matty felt weird about what Lucy was saying. Offended. He might not look like his parents, but he was like them in other ways. All three of them shared an interest in gardening. They all had pretty high IQs. And... and...

'Why don't you just tell them about me?' asked Lucy, as she replaced the photo.

'Oh no. No, no, no.' His mind was now squarely focused on *not* revealing Lucy's presence. 'Um... no! Can't do that. I mean. You're a stranger. And a girl.

And I just brought you home. Don't think they'll like that.'

Lucy hesitated, studying him intently. This made Matty feel more uncomfortable than ever. He could feel another blush spreading across his face.

After what seemed like an eternity, Lucy nodded. 'Okay then,' she said. 'We'll do it your way.'

LUCY

– CHAPTER FIVE –

SETTLING IN

Lucy was running for her life. Chased by shadows and things unseen. Her legs were aching and her lungs felt ready to burst. And although she ran and ran and ran, she didn't seem to be getting anywhere.

Above her, a meteor streaked through the darkness, its fiery glow providing sudden illumination. The things that relentlessly pursued her were getting closer, and she caught glimpses as she snatched looks over her shoulder. Strange and terrifying things. Squid-like aliens. Dinosaurs. Weird snake puppet things. Really big blue bears?

She stumbled, regained her footing and continued on towards…

Someone waited up ahead. Someone familiar. Someone who would protect her. Protect her and everyone!

But who was it?

Her eyes tried to focus on the man.

But just as he was becoming clear, there was a burst of sudden light. And it was all gone.

Lucy blinked and groaned, holding up a hand to cover her eyes. Sunlight streamed into the room. She looked about in confusion. Where was she?

'Wakey, wakey.' Matty stood by the open venetian blinds.

And then she remembered. She was in Australia, in 1985, in the spare room of some random boy, with no memories of who she was or why she was here. She groaned again and buried her face in the pillow.

'You okay?' asked Matty.

'Yeah,' Lucy mumbled into the pillow. 'Just dandy.' She desperately wanted this boy to go away so she could go back to sleep, back to her dream. She wanted to know who that man was. No... she *needed* to know. For some reason, she felt that if she could just remember who he was, she might remember everything else.

'Sorry I had to wake you.' The boy wasn't going to go away. *And* he was going to keep talking at her. 'I've been up for ages. I looked in on you when I woke up at six twenty-seven but you were still asleep.'

Six twenty-seven? Who the hell said six twenty-seven, wondered Lucy? A normal person would just say six thirty. That was close enough, surely.

'Anyway, it's now seven forty-one and I've got to get to school. My parents just left for work and I'll be back long before they get home. So you've got the house to yourself. There's food in the fridge. A radio and television in the lounge room. As well as the books in my room, there's loads more on the shelves in the lounge. I think you should watch some telly. Yeah, definitely. Especially the news. It might help you remember stuff.' He took a deep breath and headed for the door. 'Anyway, gotta go.'

And he was out the door and gone.

Things began to sink in. Matty had been wearing a uniform. Grey and boring. And now he was gone. Off to school. And she was alone. In a strange house.

Lucy threw back the musty blankets. She was still wearing yesterday's t-shirt. Sitting up she decided she needed to have a shower and find some fresh clothes.

Lucy felt human again. She'd had a shower and borrowed one of Matty's t-shirts. Feeling a little fed up with his obsession, she picked the only one that didn't have a sci-fi theme. It was dark blue with the words 'PSEUDO ECHO' and a picture of four guys with very big hair. Lucy assumed they must be a band. Now she sat in the kitchen eating something called Vita Brits. They looked and tasted a bit like

Weetabix, but not as good. She would rather have had something more sugary and less healthy-tasting.

Yet again, she found herself thinking about her lost memories. What would she do if they never came back? She couldn't just stay here, in this boy's house, hiding in the spare room. But what else could she do? *Think, think, think!* In the end, she decided all she could do for the moment was try to jog her memory.

She picked up the bowl and slurped the leftover milk before washing, drying and putting away the spoon and bowl. She wanted to be careful and not leave any indication that she was in the house.

Wandering into the lounge, she switched on the television. It was a large squarish box, grey on the front with wood panel on the sides, sitting on a corner cabinet. It had a slightly curved screen and the picture wasn't very clear. It jumped and distorted with grey fuzziness threatening it from the edges. It seemed wrong. Shouldn't the image be clearer? Shouldn't it be wider?

There were people playing some sort of football. But not proper football. Lucy turned the large knob to change the channel. Some sort of little kids' show with a lady gazing through a hand mirror. 'I can see James and Justin and Courtney and—' She quickly changed the channel again. There was someone in a large cat suit prancing about. She changed the channel again. *Sesame Street*. That was something she recognised. But she turned the knob again and was greeted by grey sizzling nothingness. Static. She turned it again. More static. She twirled the knob through the remaining clicks... but there was nothing more. Only four stations? Surely that couldn't be right. There had to be more. She tried clicking through them again. No, that was it. Just four choices of what to watch.

Leaving the television on *Sesame Street* with the sound turned down, she started to browse through the bookshelves. There were a lot of gardening books and a lot of *National Geographic* magazines and some *Reader's Digest*. On the bottom shelf she found some history and science books. She finally picked a *Reader's Digest* and settled herself on the couch to read.

She flipped through it until she came to an article about the Space Shuttle program. Apparently in February 1984, during a *Challenger* mission, one of the crew performed the first ever untethered spacewalk, using a special propulsion backpack. A jetpack in outer space!

Then Lucy frowned. There was something about the shuttle name. *Challenger*. For some reason it upset her. But she couldn't think why. Something about a teacher.

The image of an explosion blazed in Lucy's mind, and a headache took hold.

MATTY

– CHAPTER SIX –

MYSTERIOUS SYNCHRONISED HEADACHES THAT COULD MEAN SOMETHING

Matty closed his eyes. He suddenly felt headachy and a bit queasy.

He had been thinking about Lucy while trying to listen to his Maths teacher, when his mind had wandered to her question about the photo in his room and about the lack of resemblance between him and his parents… and then all of a sudden, he had this headache.

He tried taking a few deep breathes, and slowly the headache began to fade.

'Surely my class isn't so boring that it has put you

to sleep?'

Matty's eyes snapped open to reveal Mr Cronan looming over him. 'Sorry, Sir.'

'You must know all about quadratic equations if you feel you can nap rather than pay attention. So perhaps you could regale the class with your understanding.'

'Oh...' Matty straightened up in his seat. 'Sure. A quadratic equation takes the form of ax squared, plus bx, plus c, equals zero. A, b and c are known numbers but x is unknown. But that's just the standard form. There are also—'

'Yes, that's quite enough,' grumbled the teacher, obviously annoyed that his attempt to embarrass a pupil had failed.

As Mr Cronan stalked to the front of the class, a couple of the students sniggered, while someone behind Matty hissed, 'Nerd!'

There was a greater degree of tension in the room for the remainder of the Maths class, but Matty managed to make his way through it, his headache ebbing away.

Matty stumbled through the rest of the school day, distracted by thoughts of the strange girl he'd hidden in his house. What if it had all been a horrible mistake? What if she was some kind of criminal? What if she'd been robbing him and his parents while he was at school? Or what if his parents had come home unexpectedly and found her there?

These anxious thoughts swirled around his mind until the bell rang, signalling the end of classes for that day. The moment his teacher said 'Dismissed!' Matty was out the door racing for the bike shed, then peddling his hardest to get home.

He burst into the lounge, out of breath, red-faced and sweaty, to find Lucy asleep on the couch. She woke with a start, confused.

'You okay?' he asked, relieved that she hadn't been burgling the house.

'Yeah. Just having a weird dream about someone I know but can't remember.'

'Oh.' He dumped his school bag on the floor and came over to sit down beside her, as she propped herself up. 'So you've got amnesia even in your dreams.'

Lucy shook her head. 'It was just a dream. Waking memories are probably more important.'

'So how did that go?' asked Matty. 'Remember anything?'

'Sort of.' She frowned, then smiled. 'I remembered my birthday. It's the second of June.'

'Cool. Happy birthday for a couple of months ago. Get anything good?'

'Can't remember.' She looked momentarily unhappy, then perked up. 'But I remembered my parents, and my brothers... ah... Nick and... Con. And my surname is Wilson.' She paused, her brow crinkling again. 'But there's more to it than that. My name, I mean.'

'Like a middle name?' asked Matty.

'No. No, there's something else. Like... a different name... a hidden one. Oh, I dunno.'

'Anything else?' prompted Matty. 'Maybe something about where you come from?'

'I'm pretty sure I'm not from Australia.'

'Yeah, well, given your accent, we already knew that.' Matty grinned.

Lucy smiled in return.

'Want something to eat?'

'Yes,' answered Lucy. 'I'm starving.'

'Didn't you raid the fridge?' asked Matty.

'No, I forgot about lunch,' admitted Lucy. 'I watched some television and did some reading. But then I got this sudden headache. So I closed my eyes and, well, fell asleep.'

'Huh! I had a headache today too.'

'It felt weird,' said Lucy. 'Not quite like an ordinary headache. And it happened right after I had this sort of memory.'

'What do you mean?'

'I was reading about the *Challenger* space shuttle when I had this memory of an explosion. But it was like something on the television...'

'You mean like a special effect from a sci-fi show?' prompted Matty.

'No... more like news footage.'

There were a few moments of silence before Lucy looked at Matty. 'What about you? What were you doing when you got your headache?'

'I was in Maths class.'

'Yeah, well, that'd give anyone a headache.'

Matty laughed. 'I wasn't actually listening to the teacher. I was thinking about my parents.'

'Parents have been known to be headache-inducing, too.' She laughed. Matty decided he liked her laugh even more than her smile. 'Anyway, you mentioned something about food.'

Having had a snack, the kids hung out in the kitchen for a while and then went back to Matty's room before his parents came home. Telling them that he had homework (which he did, but he managed to speed through in about half an hour), he got out of spending time with them. Not that they needed his help with dinner that night, as it was Spag Bol leftovers.

'We should go to the library tomorrow and research amnesia,' suggested Matty. 'We might be able to find some information on how to trigger memories.'

'The library.' Lucy nodded slowly, then looked

at Matty, frowning as if trying to remember something. 'Wouldn't it be easier to use the computer.'

'Computer? Well, we've got a computer at school. But you need to be a member of the computer club to use it. And I don't see how it could help.'

'But...' Lucy now closed her eyes, brow furrowed, concentration etched across her face. 'The Internet!'

'The what?'

'The Internet!' Lucy opened her eyes wide, a smile breaking across her face. 'The Internet! I remember it. Sort of. Um, an information network. Computers all over the world joined together, sharing...'

But Matty wasn't listening anymore. Unfamiliar images and thoughts flashed through his mind. A web of data. Neural links. Unlimited information. He felt like he could access it. Use it.

'AAARGH!'

Lucy and Matty both cried out as pain stabbed through their heads.

'What was that?' Lucy's voice was a pained whisper, as she brought her hands up to hold her head.

'Headache,' muttered Matty, clutching his own head.

There was a knock at the door.

'You okay in there,' came Mum's worried voice.

Matty frantically gestured at the bed, and Lucy quickly scrambled under. Just as the bedroom door opened.

'I heard you yell out,' said Mum, her head peeking through a crack in the door. 'What happened?'

'Banged my head,' explained Matty.

'How'd you do that?' Mum opened the door wider and stepped in, scrutinising the room suspiciously.

'Um, I was just cleaning up.' Matty fought through the headache to come up with an explanation. 'I was shoving stuff under the bed and slipped.'

'Cleaning up?' Mum smiled. 'That's a new one.'

'Yeah, well, I'm not going to be doing any more of that.' Matty rubbed at his head. 'Got a headache now.'

'Do you want something for it?'

'Yeah.' Matty stumbled to his feet. 'Yeah, I'll come get a Disprin.'

He bundled his mum out of the room, closing the door behind him. He fetched himself a tablet, popped it into some water and watched it dissolve in a frenzied fizz, then downed it in two gulps. He rinsed the glass, refilled it and dropped another tablet in, carrying it back to his room.

'You can come out now,' he said.

Lucy slid out from under the bed, and he held out the medicine to her.

'That was weird.' Lucy drained the glass and screwed up her face at the taste. 'Both our heads at the same time.' She paused. 'I wonder if our earlier headaches were synchronised as well.'

'Twelve twenty-eight for me,' said Matty.

'I don't know what time it was,' said Lucy. 'But it was just as I was starting to get hungry for lunch.'

'Something odd is going on.' Matty sat down on the floor next to Lucy. 'Maybe it's linked to your memories.'

'I don't know. I didn't get any headaches from remembering my family.'

'Hmmm, maybe there are some specific repressed memories that trigger it?'

'But why are you getting the headaches too?'

'Maybe we're linked somehow.' He got to his feet, his headache fading. 'We are definitely going to the library.'

He made up his mind. Tomorrow, he'd ditch school and spend the day with Lucy. He was already taking Thursday and Friday off school to go to the convention, so what was one more day? And working out this mystery was way more important than school anyway.

LUCY

– CHAPTER SEVEN –

FISH AND CHIPS

Lucy was running for her life. Again. She was being chased by all manner of things. Creatures. Aliens. Robots.

Up ahead was someone who could stop them all. Who could save her. He had grey hair, a wrinkled face with a moustache, and eyes that were both kind and determined. And she knew him.

He was…

'Wakey, wakey!'

'No,' Lucy protested into her pillow. 'Aaargh!'

Was this going to happen every morning? Being woken just before she found out who the man was. Maybe she could go back to sleep. Go back to the dream.

'Go away, Hobo,' she mumbled.

'Hobo?' Matty's voice was puzzled. 'I'm not a hobo. Is that meant to be some kind of insult?'

'What? No.' Lucy lifted her head from the pillow and stared, bleary-eyed, at the boy by the window, sunlight shining through the blinds and onto his hair, making him seem like he was glowing. Hair? 'Hobo is a person. Someone I know. Someone without any hair.'

'A bald hobo? Okay.' Matty's voice sounded dubious.

'Damnit!' Lucy hit her fist into her pillow. 'I should know who he is. I feel like he's... important to me.'

'Maybe a shower and some breakfast will help,' suggested Matty.

'I suppose so.' Lucy continued to stare at her pillow, mind ticking over, trying to remember.

'Come on.' Matty's voice broke into her thoughts. 'You don't want to stay here all day. It's already nine thirty-two. My parents are long gone and I've rung my school to let them know I'm sick.' He lowered his voice. 'I think I did a good job of imitating my dad on the phone.' He cleared his throat and returned to his normal voice. 'You should have that shower and breakfast, then we can head out.'

'Out?'

'Yeah, out! We need to go to the library. Plus, I thought it might be a good idea to just wander around a bit. Hopefully that might jog some memories for you.'

Lucy sighed. 'Okay.'

With a spray of gravel, Lucy brought the bike to a stop and grinned at Matty. At least she hadn't forgotten how to ride. That was something to be happy about. She was using Matty's mum's bicycle, which had been sitting disused in the spare room she had been sleeping in. She had another of Matty's t-shirts on, but the *Star Wars* logo was hidden beneath her hoodie. She had made Matty put her own t-shirt into the wash so she would be able to have it back tomorrow.

'So, why are we here?' asked Lucy. 'I thought we were going to the library.'

'Doesn't open until eleven.'

Leaving the bikes in the rack at the end of the car park, they followed a short path down to the beach.

'Port Phillip Bay,' announced Matty, as he trod out onto the sand, arm cutting an arc through the air, indicating the expanse of wavy blue ahead of them. 'Opens out onto Bass Strait beyond The Rip.' He pointed out into the distance where the water met the dark clouds. 'Not that you can see it from here.' He turned to the brick building at the edge of the sand to their right. 'That's the Mentone Life Saving Club. Established in 1920.'

'You applying for a tour guide job or something?' asked Lucy, with a snort.

'Is there a beach where you live?' asked Matty, ignoring her snarky comment and continuing to gaze out to sea.

'Yes.'

'Ah-ha!' He whirled around to face her, pointing a finger at her nose. 'You just remembered something.'

She smacked his hand away, then smiled. 'I guess I did. In fact... I think we live near a beach.' She paused. 'The Sea. The town is by the sea. I can see... the sea. From the house.' She nodded. 'Yeah. I can picture my house. I can picture the view. And there's this rock out in the water. It's covered at high tide. And it's... it's...'

'It's what?"

Lucy stopped herself from saying 'it's haunted'. That was just too crazy. Instead, she just shrugged. And yet, she felt sure that this rock in the water that she could see from her house was, indeed, haunted.

'I reckon we've just got to go on talking about things. And looking around at stuff and places. And... anything really. You never know what might spark a memory.'

Lucy nodded.

Matty nodded back at her.

And then they fell into an awkward silence.

'So...' began Lucy.

'So...' responded Matty.

They both looked out at the bay, little waves gently rolling onto the shore. It was fairly calm and there was a smattering of yachts and other boats out on the water. Despite the chilly weather there were even a few swimmers out there.

'Do you like swimming?'

'Maybe... I think.'

Lucy shifted her attention to the Mentone Life Saving club. The building had a flat roof with a railing that ran around the perimeter. It was probably used as a look-out area. And sure enough, there was someone up there, looking out. Looking in their direction. White hair. Grey clothes. Sunglasses despite the overcast weather. Could it be that woman from the train? Surely not! That would be too much of a coincidence.

Beep, beep, beep.

Lucy's attention was distracted as Matty checked his watch and pressed a button. 'Time to go. We should get to the library just as it's opening.'

She turned back to the Life Saving Club, but the person was gone.

'Loss of memory, most often as a result of trauma to the brain. Examples of trauma include stroke, infection, Alzheimer's disease, alcohol, emotional shock...' Matty's voice fell away as his finger ran down the encyclopaedia entry.

'So basically, I have brain damage,' said Lucy, seated next to him in the library. 'Any more great news?'

'It says here that amnesia can last days, weeks, months or even years.'

'This just gets better and better.' Lucy leaned forward on the table and put her head in her hands. Years? That was a depressing thought.

'Amnesia can be anterograde or retrograde,' Matty continued reading.

'And what does that mean?'

'Anterograde means that you forget events after the trauma. And retrograde means you forget events before the trauma.' Matty paused and looked up to meet Lucy's eyes. 'Since you can't remember anything before I found you in the bookshop, you must have retrograde amnesia.'

'So something traumatic happened in the bookshop?'

'Maybe.' Matty scratched his chin. 'But you were unconscious when I found you. So the trauma might have happened somewhere else. And then you were brought to the bookshop.' He continued to scratch at his chin. 'But how did you get into the bookshop? You would have had to go right past me to get up to that room,' he mumbled, almost to himself. 'Did someone sneak you in, maybe?'

'What if…' Lucy stopped. She was about to

suggest something that any reasonable person would find completely ridiculous, and yet, for some reason, she didn't think it was ridiculous at all. She actually seemed to think it was a real possibility. She wondered why she would be so easily accepting of such an outlandish idea.

'Yeah?' prompted Matty.

'What if I was, somehow, instantaneously transported into that room?' She held up her hand to stop Matty, in case he was going to object. 'Just hear me out. And however it happened, it caused the trauma that made me forget.'

'You mean, like, teleporting or something?' Matty's eyes were wide with excitement. He obviously didn't think it was ridiculous either. 'Or it could have been a wormhole? Both of which could have scrambled your brain a bit. Or...' He paused, nodding to himself enthusiastically. 'Time travel!'

'Time travel...' Lucy whispered the words. They felt... familiar.

'It makes sense.' Matty was still nodding to himself. 'If you're from the future, it would explain why you reckon a computer could be used to research amnesia. Sometimes countries change names, so it would explain why things in the atlas seemed wrong to you. And why you thought the train ticket was so cheap, but that the train was so noisy.' He tilted his head to the side and stared at her. 'That's it. You're from the future. A future where computers are commonplace and trains are silent and everything is really expensive. And you being taken out of your own time is the trauma that caused your amnesia.'

Strangely, it all made sense to Lucy. 'You know what, I think you might be right.'

'You're amazing!' declared Matty, then he turned away quickly, face reddening. 'I mean this is amazing. This situation. You. Bookshop. Appearing out of nowhere. It's like something out of a science fiction book. Only it's real. Time travel!'

'Time travel!' echoed Lucy.

'Do you like fish and chips?' called Matty, peddling up alongside Lucy on his bike.

'Yes. Yes I do. I remember eating them when Mum and Dad and I'd just moved to... somewhere... by the sea.' Lucy grinned. 'I actually remember! And they were fantastic!'

'So you have fish and chips in the future, then?'

'I guess we must.' Lucy laughed, exhilarated by the wind in her face, the anticipation of lunch and the thought of time travel.

'This way!' Matty pulled ahead and led them across the railway line and towards a small set of shops.

They came to a stop outside a milk bar that had

a sign in the window with the words 'Fish & Chips' surrounded by blinking lights. Going inside, Matty dug a hand into his pocket and pulled out a few coins. 'I'm afraid it's just going to be chips.'

'I'll live.'

A large woman in a flowery caftan ambled out from the back of the shop in response to the tinkling of the bell above the door.

As Matty ordered minimum chips and handed over fifty cents worth of coins, Lucy watched with a puzzled expression.

'Too cheap, future-girl?' asked Matty.

'That and the whole cents things.'

'It's pounds and pence in the UK, isn't it?' said Matty. 'Not dollars and cents.'

They sat themselves down on the rickety chairs in the corner of the milk bar as the lady disappeared into the back of the shop to cook the chips.

'I want to find out more about time travel,' said Lucy. 'Like, proper science stuff, not science fiction. Too bad there was nothing in the library.'

'It's a small public library,' said Matty. 'We could try the State Library. It's got lots more books. And there's this massive room with a dome where you can go to read.'

'Sounds cool.'

'Or we could go talk to Marvin.'

'Marvin?'

'He's the guy who owns Space/Time Books,' said Matty. 'Remember? You met him on the way out.'

'That weird guy who liked my ring?' Lucy's fingers automatically felt for the ring, making sure it was still there.

'That's him. But there's more to him than you first think. He knows things. About science and stuff. He reckons that there's a whole lot of science fiction that's based on science fact. And so he's got a whole science section in the bookshop.'

'Okay then,' said Lucy. 'Let's go talk to him.'

'Can't do that today.' Matty sighed and leaned back on the chair. 'Shop's closed 'cause he's getting ready for Aussiecon.'

'You know, sometimes you don't make much sense.'

'Sorry. Aussiecon Two starts tomorrow. It's the forty-third World Science Fiction Convention and it's being held here in Melbourne.' Lucy saw his eyes light up. 'There's five days worth of panels and talks and author signings and dealers and...'

'Okay, okay,' said Lucy, interrupting him. 'I get it. Big sci-fi thing. You're excited.'

'And Marvin's got a dealer's table in the hucksters' room.'

'Right. So you want to go talk to him there?'

'Yeah,' said Matty. 'I mean, I'm going to Aussiecon anyway. I've got a membership and my parents even gave me permission to miss some school in order to go.' He stopped and frowned. 'But you won't be able to get in without a member badge.'

'Can't we buy another ticket?'

'They're like, fifty dollars or something.'

'Is that a lot, is it?'

'Um, yeah. My parents paid for mine.' Matty looked up as the lady came out from the back, carrying their order. 'But we'll work something out.'

Steam seeped out from the edges of the paper as the lady dropped the bundle of wrapped chips onto the table.

'Thanks,' said Lucy.

'No worries, love,' she answered, before heading back to the counter.

Matty ripped a hole in the paper, dug out a chip and popped it into his mouth. Then he immediately yelped and started bouncing in his chair, flapping his arms around and breathing, 'Hot! Hot! Hot!'

Lucy giggled. This guy was such a dork. And yet kind of nice.

She decided to let the chips cool down a bit before digging in. Instead, her mind drifted back to her situation. 'I wonder how I did it?' she mused.

'Did what?'

'Travel in time.' It still amazed her that she could say these words and actually believe them.

'Oh.' He managed to swallow his chip. 'You

mean like, did you have a time machine? Or was it a random anomaly?' He paused, his hand hovering over the tear in the chip wrapping. 'Did you mean to travel back in time? Or was it an accident? Or a temporal kidnapping?' He frowned, his hand dropping to the table, the chips forgotten. 'Maybe you had no choice. Maybe something happened in your own time and you were whisked off into the past. Against… against your will.'

Lucy tried to think about what might have happened to her, but her mind was a blank. Matty, on the other hand, continued talking, he eyes suddenly distant.

'Maybe your life was in danger. Maybe other people's lives were threatened. Danger. Death. Destruction. And…'

'ARGGGGGGHHH!'

Lucy clutched her head.

'No worries, love.'

'Hot! Hot! Hot!'

'I wonder how I did it?'

'Maybe you had no choice.'

'Danger. Death. Destruction.'

'ARGGGGGGHHH!'

Lucy clutched her head. Through squinted eyes she could see Matty doing the same. Pain stabbed at her mind. She held her breath and clenched her teeth.

'No worries, love.'

'Hot! Hot! Hot!'

'I wonder how I did it?'

'Maybe you had no choice.'

'Danger. Death. Destruction.'

'ARGGGGGGHHH!'

Lucy clutched her head. Through squinted eyes she could see Matty doing the same. Pain stabbed at her mind. She held her breath and clenched her teeth. She closed her eyes.

And it passed into a dull throb.

She let out her breath and slowly opened her eyes.

Matty was slumped over the table. His face was planted in the chips.

'Flamin' heck! Are you okay?' The milk bar owner was rushing towards them, her face white with alarm.

Matty groaned.

'Glass of water!' It came out more like an order than a request. Lucy tried to soften it by adding 'Please.'

As the lady ran off, Lucy hopped out of her chair and lifted Matty up from the chips. He groaned.

'Ow. My head.'

'Are you okay?' asked Lucy.

'Yeah. I think.'

'Here you go, love.' The milk bar owner was back with a glass of water held out with trembling hands.

Lucy looked up in response, to see a face staring

at them through the shop window. A face with white hair and dark glasses. It was that woman from the train. So she *had* been watching them at the beach!

And then she was gone.

'Back in a moment,' called Lucy, bolting for the door.

She made it outside just in time to see the woman disappearing down a small alley. Without a second thought, Lucy gave chase, trainers slapping on the pavement as she ran. Slowing down as she rounded the corner, Lucy saw the woman racing out the other end into a vacant lot overgrown with grass and weeds.

Lucy put on a burst of speed and entered the lot just as the woman jumped onto the fence at the end of the property and started to clamber. Lucy was certain she had her now, but her progress was hampered by knee-high grass and weeds, and some sort of low-lying, thorny creeper that caught at her feet and ankles.

'Ow,' cried Lucy, as the thorns scratched her legs.

She kicked out at them and stomped on the creeper vines. And the next thing she knew, she was toppling over, ankles wrapped in vegetation. She struggled to get to her feet, her hands and arms somehow managing to get tangled in the weeds. By the time she managed to extricate herself, pulling up great clumps of grass in the process, the woman was over the fence. But Lucy stumbled on, fighting against the greenery. Finally reaching the fence, she climbed up and looked over.

It was someone's backyard, an expanse of neatly edged lawn and immaculately planted flowerbeds. But there was no sign of the mystery woman.

MATTY

– CHAPTER EIGHT –

FREAKY REPEATING BITS OF TIME

Matty's head pounded. What in the world had just happened? He tried to calm himself. Gulping down the water, he handed back the glass.

'Are you all right now, love?' asked the milk bar owner.

'Yeah, I'm fine.' Matty gave her a weak smile. He wasn't really fine at all. His head still throbbed and he was feeling slightly nauseous. He gave her a wan smile. 'It was just a really sudden headache.'

'Sounds like it might have been a migraine,' suggested the woman as she shuffled off, nodding to herself. 'You should get your parents to take you to the doctor.'

'Yeah, I'll do that.'

The shop bell tinkled to announce Lucy's return.

'Where did you go?' asked Matty.

'First,' said Lucy, plonking down onto the chair.

'Are you okay now?'

'Still got a headache. But that intense stab of pain is gone.' He smiled weakly.

'Good.' But there was still concern in her eyes. 'You remember that woman from the train?'

'The one who was asleep?' Matty was confused. Why was Lucy bringing this up now?

'She wasn't asleep.' There was a hint of annoyance in her voice. 'I thought I saw her when we were at the beach. At the lifesaving club. And then she was just here staring at us through the window.' Lucy jerked a thumb back over her shoulder.

'Are you sure?'

'Yes, I'm sure.' She was definitely irritated now.

'Okay, okay. Sorry. I believe you.' He took a deep breath as his mind ran through everything that had happened. 'You think she's connected to the headaches?'

Lucy shrugged. 'I really don't know. But it's a bit suspicious that she's following us.' She reached out to the paper on the table between them and picked up a squashed chip, studied it for a moment, then dropped it back down.

Matty grimaced. 'Sorry about that.'

'Yeah!' said Lucy in mock outrage. 'How dare you collapse into the chips!'

It broke the tension and they both laughed.

The milk bar owner shuffled over with a new wrapped bundle that she dumped onto the table, gathering up the old one. 'Brought you some more chips. And I popped a couple of potato cakes in there too.'

'Thanks!' Matty and Lucy said in unison as she traipsed off.

Matty ripped open the new packet, grabbed a chip and popped it into his mouth. He yelped and started bouncing in his chair, flapping his arms around and breathing, 'Hot! Hot! Hot!', just like he had done earlier.

'OMG!' whispered Lucy.

Matty fussed a little more before finally chewing and swallowing the chip. Then he noticed Lucy's stunned expression. 'What?'

'When the headache, or whatever it was, happened, did you feel anything else?'

'Yes,' he said tentatively. He *had* experienced something strange – well, stranger than just the sudden pain in his head. But he had assumed he had just imagined it.

'Did things kind of repeat?' continued Lucy, almost bouncing in her chair.

'Yes!' This time his answer was more emphatic. That was exactly what had happened to him. His heart thudded in his chest, a kind of excited trepidation taking hold of him and slowly squeezing. 'It was like some sort of a flashback. It happened twice.'

Lucy was nodding frantically. 'Like images over the top of the pain.'

'Yeah. Like time repeating itself.'

That was a lot to take in. Matty ate another chip, this time ignoring the heat and just chomping down on it. He watched as Lucy also took a chip. Since meeting this girl two days ago, he'd gone from reading science fiction to living it.

He regarded her, eating chips across the table from him, and began to wonder. Was she the problem? Was she causing this? His life had been devastatingly normal and boring up until she showed up. He'd hardly ever had a headache before meeting her, let alone sudden, sharp stabbing pains that almost made him pass out. And now repeating bits of time. Freaky!

Who was she? What was she doing to him?

'You okay?' Lucy was waving a hand in front of his face.

'Oh. Yeah. Just thinking.'

'Over there!' Lucy took off.

Matty peddled hard, trying desperately to keep up. She could certainly ride fast when she wanted to.

After they had finished their chips in an

awkward silence, thoughts of Lucy being a potential danger whirling through Matty's head, Lucy had insisted they check the surrounding streets for the mystery woman.

It was another false alarm – just a woman in similar clothes, but definitely not who they were searching for. Not that Matty was all that certain of what she looked like. He hadn't really taken that much notice of her on the train. It was Lucy who was driving this futile search. And so Matty followed along, trying to work out what he should do.

He could talk to Lucy and try to convince her to go to the police? They might be able to find out who she really was. But he didn't really think she'd go for that.

Maybe he could talk to his parents? Tell them everything that had happened and let them sort it out for him. But he wasn't some little kid. He was fifteen. He should be able to take care of his own problems. Shouldn't he? Besides, if he told his parents, he'd probably get into serious trouble for bringing Lucy home with him in the first place. And for hiding her.

Perhaps he should just ditch her? She probably didn't remember the way home and even if she did, she didn't have a key.

Matty sighed guiltily.

He couldn't do that to her. After all, he had been

the one to suggest she stay with him. Why in the world had he done it?

Lucy took off again. Matty struggled to keep up. Then Lucy shouted something and put on another burst of speed. Matty tried to see ahead of her. There was someone there. Running. Weaving through passers-by, then across the street, dodging cars. Trying to get away. Could it be?

Matty somehow managed to find an extra reserve of strength and forced his legs to peddle faster. Lucy was gaining on her quarry, and he was gaining on her. It was a woman with white hair in a grey coat, just like Lucy had described. Well, if they caught up to her, maybe they would find out what was going on.

But the woman raced across another road, just ahead of an onslaught of traffic. Lucy came to a halt with a squeak of brakes and Matty almost crashed into her, stopping only just in time.

'She's… heading for the… beach.' Lucy was out a breath, but as soon as the cars cleared, she was off again. Matty had no option but to follow.

Abandoning the bikes, Matty and Lucy chased the woman onto the sand. After all the frenetic bike riding, running through the soft sand, his feet sinking into it with each step, was super hard. And the sand getting into his sneakers didn't make things any easier.

Matty saw the woman glance over her shoulder as they drew closer. Then she stopped as if coming to a decision, pulling at her left sleeve.

'Gotchya!' cried Lucy.

Matty stumbled as he ran and fell face first into the sand.

'Gotchya!' cried Lucy.

Matty stumbled as he ran and fell face first into the sand.

What had happened?

Matty looked up to see Lucy ahead.

Had he fallen twice?

He looked down at the sand, shook his head and looked up again. Lucy was walking in circles with wide-eyed confusion. The woman was nowhere to be seen.

Staggering to his feet, Matty approached Lucy.

'She's gone!' Lucy kicked at the beach in frustration, sending a spray of sand into the air. 'One moment she was there. And then she wasn't.' She kicked again sending a spray of sand into the air. 'She's gone!'

As Matty watched, the particles seemed to hang in the air just a little too long. On instinct, he whirled around to look back to where their bikes were... just in time to see a blur of motion.

As they rode the bikes towards home, finally having

admitted defeat, they passed through the little group of shops where they had eaten chips in the milk bar. They peddled up the street and across the railway line, the sand between his toes irritating Matty with each movement of his feet.

'Is there an army base or something around here?' asked Lucy, as she came up alongside him.

'No. Why?'

Lucy indicated the jeep that was approaching them. Matty could see the green-coloured uniforms of the people inside.

The vehicle raced past, crossed the railway line and headed for the shops.

'Even soldiers need to shop, I guess,' said Matty, returning his attention to the road ahead. But it made him uneasy. He'd never seen military personnel of any kind around his neighbourhood before. Was it coincidence? Or was it somehow connected with this strange girl, the woman who'd been following them and the weird things that were happening?

'I fell twice.' Matty was lying on his bed watching Lucy pace the room. 'I mean… I fell once… but it happened twice. And then everything slowed down. Just for a moment.'

'Are you sure?' she said, coming to a stop and staring intently at him.

'Yes.'

'Weird!' She resumed pacing. ''Cause I didn't feel anything like that.'

'So, how did she disappear?' Matty propped himself up on an elbow. 'Did she have some kind of device or machine or something? Did you see anything? And did you actually see her disappear? Like, did she fade away? Or what?'

'That's the odd bit. I don't remember.' Lucy stopped again. 'It's almost like I looked away and when I looked back, she was gone. Except that I didn't actually look away.' She frowned. 'At least I don't think I did.'

'It was some kind of time distortion.' Matty sat up, bouncing on the end of his bed. He marvelled again at how science fiction was becoming his lived experience. 'After it happened. After she was gone and you were all upset. I glanced back to where our bikes were and I thought I saw something. Just a movement really. And I reckon it was her.'

Lucy had a doubtful expression. He took a deep breath and ploughed on.

'There was this book I read once. And the hero in it was able to mess with time in small ways. It was called a localised time distortion. He would use it to escape from the bad guys. Time would distort, slowing down or repeating for the people chasing him, and he could just run off. When the time flow returned to normal, he was long gone.' He took another deep breath. 'I reckon that's what happened to us. That's how she escaped.'

'So you think she can control time?' Lucy was staring at him now.

'Yes,' said Matty. 'And if she can control time, you know what that means?'

'Yeah.' Lucy nodded slowly. 'It means she's probably how I got here.'

LUCY

– CHAPTER NINE –

AUSSIECON TWO

Lucy was running for her life. Yet again. Things bared their fangs in occasional flashes of light that punctuated the darkness around her. She could feel the menace and malice radiating from them, threatening to envelop her.

And again… there he was. The oh-so-familiar man with the kind yet determined eyes. The man who could make everything safe and comfortable and familiar. He made her think of home and warmth and cuddles and…

She almost had it. She could sense the memory of who he was, tantalisingly dancing just beyond her perception. As she came nearer to him, his lips moved.

What was he saying?

It was a name.

Her name.

'Lucyloo.'

She opened her arms wide and reached out towards him...

BANG!

Lucy woke with a start, jumping up out of bed ready to defend herself against...

Nothing!

The dim light of dawn was seeping its way into the room through the Venetian blinds. She staggered over to the window and peered through the blinds, quickly ducking back when she saw a man in a faded blue dressing gown carrying a metal bin. It was Matty's dad. She settled back down onto the mattress.

Even without Matty waking her, it seemed like she was destined never to learn the identity of the man in her dream. And she had been so close. He was so familiar. So... comfortable. A relative, maybe?

Lucy found the whole memory thing so difficult to wrap her mind around. She remembered certain basic things about her family — her mother's name was Tamara and her dad's was Albert; her brothers were Nick and Conall; she had cousins, didn't she? — but not the context. She was sure that she loved her family, but she couldn't find any specifics of her relationships with them. How well did she get along with her parents? Did they understand and support her? Did they argue? She just didn't know.

She closed her eyes and listened to the

movements in the house beyond the spare room. Sounds of footsteps, clinking dishes, a shower – the daily routine of getting ready for school and work. She suddenly felt all choked up and teary. It was the absence of ordinary, everyday family things from her memories that made her sad. She rubbed at her eyes, determined not to cry.

Did she have a daily routine? She must have. She went to school. She knew that. But… where was that school? Did she wear a uniform? Did she like her teachers? What subjects did she study? Did she have friends?

A vision of a bald head flashed into her mind.

Hobo?

She knew this boy. This friend. Did they go to school together?

She tried to focus on him. He wasn't just bald, was he? He had no hair at all. No eyebrows. And he… he did something with words? And…

And then it was gone.

Every time memories seemed like they were coming back, they would slip away again. It was very frustrating.

She sighed and continued listening to the morning movements of Matty and his parents. She wondered what time it was. She didn't have a watch and there was no clock in the room. She smiled as she remembered how Matty had come into the room on the previous mornings, announcing the time to the exact minute. He loved his digital watch and was always glancing at it.

I bet he'd love a smart watch, she thought. And then she screwed up her face in confusion. What in the world was a smart watch?

'But my name's not Fred,' complained Lucy, waving around the plastic-encased membership badge. 'I don't exactly look like a Fred, you know.'

'It'll be fine,' Matty assured her. 'I don't think anyone actually checks the names on the badges. So long as you're wearing one, that's all that matters.'

The two teenagers were standing outside the Southern Cross Hotel, city traffic zooming past them on Exhibition Street. Matty had been inside to pick up his convention registration pack, which included his membership badge. He had also collected his best friend's pack. Fred's parents had only allowed him to take one day off school, so Matty had offered to collect his pack and give it to him when they met up on Friday to go in together. That way, Fred wouldn't have to waste time standing in the registration queue. Of course, it also meant that Lucy could use his membership badge on the Thursday.

Matty pinned his badge to the front of his jacket and stuffed the registration packs into his backpack. 'If anyone actually questions you about it, just say that Fred is short for Winifred.'

'Fine.' Lucy pinned the badge to her hoodie, not seeming at all convinced.

'Let's go!' Matty led the way into the hotel.

Lucy immediately recognised R2D2. The remote control replica was trundling around the cream-carpeted foyer, a man dressed as Obi-Wan Kenobi following it around with a control unit. She was pleased that she could remember *Star Wars*. But she wasn't sure about the other costumes she saw. There were people in robes and cloaks, someone had pointy elf ears, and there was this one guy with a really bad, fake head attached to his shoulder.

Mind you not everyone was in costume. There were lots of people simply wearing t-shirts with book titles, quotes, film posters and logos. One very large bearded guy had *Duck Dodgers in the 24 ½ th Century* emblazoned across his chest. Lucy just thought it resembled that cartoon duck her dad liked, but in a silly outfit, although she couldn't remember his name.

Matty stopped and unzipped his jacket to proudly display his t-shirt – *The Tomorrow People* in a weird font, stark white on black fabric. Lucy was very glad to be back in her own plain t-shirt, concealed under her hoodie. She gave him a pitying look.

'What?' demanded Matty. 'T-shirts are important. Especially at events like this. They display who you are as a fan. Your fictional affiliations and interests.'

'Sure.'

She thought he was about to launch into yet more declarations on the importance of t-shirts, but then he seemed to reconsider. 'This way.' He headed off upstairs. 'I think.'

Climbing the stairs, Lucy gaped at a couple who passed them on the way down. The woman was in a red uniform, part of her face ripped off to reveal reptilian scales beneath. The man's clothes were all torn and bloodied, his face and arms covered in oozing gashes. These people really took their cosplay seriously. The makeup on both of them was incredible.

On the mezzanine level, they passed more people, not all in costuming of equal quality. A woman with pointy rubber ears made a weird gesture at them with her hand as they passed, mumbling, 'Live long and prosper.'

Matty led the way along a corridor to a set of three rooms at the end. They stuck their heads into the first room. It was packed with trestle tables. Each had a sign or banner hanging down in front of it, some professionally printed, others hand-painted, with the name of the shop or a description of the merchandise being sold. The tables held an assortment of stuff, everything from books to VHS tapes; badges to posters; t-shirts to soundtrack albums.

'Not in here,' said Matty, leading the way to the end room.

More tables. More merchandise. And a scattering of people wandering around, checking things out. A man wearing pyjamas and a dressing gown, displaying a large badge with the words 'MOSTLY HARMLESS', pushed past them as they entered.

'Over there!' Matty took Lucy's hand and made his way through the people to a table in the far corner where Marvin sat, head down, engrossed in a book. 'SPACE/TIME BOOKS' said the sign on the front of the table. Lucy noticed there was a corkboard propped up on a chair behind him and pinned to it were a few Polaroid photos of people at his stall. It seemed that he had brought his hobby with him. He looked up as they approached, grinning at them.

'G'day Matty and not-Matty's-girlfriend,' he said, eyes going straight to their clasped hands.

Lucy felt the heat rise to her cheeks and immediately snatched her hand back.

'Oh... um... ah... sorry,' stammered Matty.

'Soooo...' began Marvin after an awkward silence that went on far too long. 'Ya wanna buy something?' He gave them an even bigger grin and spread his arms out wide to indicate all the books and comics displayed on the table. 'Lots of stuff to choose from. I know what you're into, Matty, but what about...'

'Lucy,' Matty filled in for him.

'Lucy,' repeated Marvin, thoughtfully. 'Lucy in the sky with diamonds. Nice song. Nice name. I think you could use a copy of...' He picked up a book and held it out. '...*The Hitchhiker's Guide to the Galaxy*. It's got an android named Marvin in it. Worth reading just for that. Written by Douglas Adams.' He glanced back at his corkboard and sighed.

'Not in your collection yet?' asked Matty.

'No, not yet. I've gotta wait a few more years for a book he hasn't written yet, so that he can come to Melbourne on tour to promote it. Then I'll get him to visit my bookshop for a signing and... SNAP! I'll take his pic.' He paused to stroke his goatee, eyes glazing over. 'Maybe get his fingerprints. Sample of his hair, perhaps. Or perchance even some of his...' Marvin suddenly raised an eyebrow. 'But enough about that.' He waved the book at her. 'How about the book? Wanna buy it?'

'No thanks.' Lucy shook her head, wondering how this weird man could possibly be of any help. Did he know anything worthwhile about time travel? 'Actually, we're here to ask you a question,' she said tentatively, nudging Matty with her elbow.

'Um, yeah, that's right,' Matty agreed.

'Oh.' Looking rather disappointed, Marvin dropped *The Hitchhiker's Guide to the Galaxy* back onto the table in front of him. 'If you must.'

'Time travel. We wanted to ask what you know about time travel.'

'Well now.' Marvin stroked his beard again, this time his eyes going wide and manic. Lucy thought he looked like some evil genius from an over-the-top spy movie. 'As it happens, I know quite a bit. So you're gonna have to be a tad more specific. Into the past? Into the future? Books? TV? Feature films? Science fiction or fantasy? Etc, etc...'

'No, no, no.' Matty shook his head. 'Not fiction. What do you know about real time travel?'

Marvin squinted at them, grimaced and crossed his arms. 'Not possible!'

'But...' started Matty.

'Yet,' continued Marvin. 'Not possible, yet! There are, however, lots of theories. Some scientists, of course, believe it to be completely impossible. They're the ones with closed minds. Not a good look for people supposedly expanding the frontiers of knowledge, if you ask me. Others believe it's theoretically possible, but unlikely, and that if it were ever to be achieved it would result in the total annihilation of... well... everything. Ka-blam! There are a small number who genuinely think it might be achievable, albeit with certain caveats, and an even smaller number who actively pursue its study. Of course, Einstein thought that time was an illusion and relative to the individual. So if you were to approach the speed of light, time would move slower for you. Thus you would, essentially, travel into the future beyond where you would naturally have ended up. But that's just slowed down time and not actual time travel, and I assume that is not what you're asking about. You want to know about proper time travel. The pick-a-point-on-the-time-line-and-go-to-it-immediately sort of time travel. Am I right? Eh? Eh? Eh?'

Matty nodded while Lucy stared at this strange man who was talking at a million miles an hour with such intense conviction.

'Again, lot of theories on how this could be achieved. Using a black hole, an infinite cylinder or cosmic strings seem the most plausible ways of achieving it. But none of those things are all that easy to come by. There is the theory of creating a time machine using negative density energy, but no one's yet been able to produce negative density energy, let alone a machine that uses it. And the only other feasible option then is the donut theory.'

Lucy gave him a sceptical glare.

'Not an actual donut,' said Marvin, raising his eyes skyward for a second and letting out a huff. 'Sheesh! I mean using gravitational fields to bend space/time in on itself to form a donut shape. Once you have that—'

'Stop!' Lucy blurted out. Then, lowering her voice, 'Please. Just stop. This is hurting my head.'

'Yeah,' agreed Matty. 'This is all way beyond us.'

'You did ask.' Marvin shrugged. 'There's a reason I called my shop Space/Time Books.' And with that, he returned to the novel he'd been reading – *The End of Eternity* by Isaac Asimov.

Lucy looked at Matty.

Matty looked at Lucy.

They both shrugged at the same time, then turned back to Marvin.

'What about the future?' asked Matty.

'What about it?'

'Do you think it's possible that time travel will be invented in the future?' asked Lucy.

'And that someone from the future could visit us?' added Matty.

'Too right!' Marvin snapped his book closed with a bang. 'If time travel is theoretically possible, then I reckon it's inevitable.' There was a distinct gleam in his eyes now. 'Why? Have you met someone from the future?'

Lucy and Matty turned to each other again. Matty

gave her a 'should we tell him' look and she responded with a little nod.

'Well…' Matty began. 'We think that Lucy is from the future.'

MATTY

– CHAPTER TEN –

TESTING THE TIME TRAVEL THEORY

Matty hoped that Marvin would believe him. The bookshop owner certainly seemed to be listening with rapt attention as Matty explained his theory about Lucy and time travel and amnesia. Lucy then jumped in, telling him about the sudden headaches and weird repeating moments.

When they finished, Marvin stroked his beard again, grinning as broadly as the Cheshire cat. Then he reached under the table. Pulling out a battered old Polaroid camera, he pointed it at Lucy and Matty.

FLASH!

'Yikes!' Matty blinked several times as he tried to clear his vision.

'Why did you do that?' demanded Lucy.

Marvin snatched up the little Polaroid rectangle as it whirred out of the front of the camera, and then waved it about in the air in Lucy's general direction. 'If you really are from the future, then I want a photo of you.' He turned around and pinned the rectangle to the corkboard behind him.

Matty stared at the photo. It was mostly blank still, shapes and colours only just beginning to form, slowly coming into existence.

'So you believe us?' said Lucy, excitedly. 'You think I could be from the future?'

'Who knows?' Marvin stowed the camera back under the table. 'Without any sort of time machine, there's no real proof. And without any definite memories, you're really just guessing, aren't ya?'

Matty saw Lucy's face fall. He hated seeing her so disappointed. It was his fault, he decided, for having built up her hopes, for bringing her to Marvin with so many expectations.

'You need to stop guessing,' said Marvin. 'You need to test your theory. That's what scientists do. They test their theories.'

'How do we do that?' asked Matty.

'Isn't it obvious?' asked Marvin. 'Jeez Louise! You try to bring on another time-jarring headache.'

'What?' Matty and Lucy cried out in unison. Heads turned and people stared.

'What-what?' Marvin got to his feet. 'Just give it a shot.' He moved the corkboard from the chair and stepped aside, indicating the two seats. 'Please be seated. I'll stand and observe.'

'Out here?' asked Lucy.

'With everyone watching?' added Matty.

'No one's watching,' Marvin assured them. 'They're all too busy spending money at tables other than mine. Which is daft given that I've got the best selection and the best prices, but that's beside the current point. The thing is, with people around you, moving about, it'll be easier to see the effects of a time distortion. So. Sit!'

Matty and Lucy obeyed, plonking themselves down on the uncomfortable foldout chairs, Matty tossing his backpack under the table.

'Okay, Lucy!' Marvin was gleefully rubbing his hands together like a kid about to get into a whole heap of mischief. 'Based on what you've told me, I reckon you need to try to remember the future.'

Remember the future, thought Matty. *What a weird thing to say.*

'Focus on anything that you can remember – people, places, things. Anything at all.'

'Uh-huh.' Lucy closed here eyes. 'There's this man that I sort of remember. I think he's the key to it all. But I don't know who he is. I can picture him. And I know I should know him, but...'

'Good, good,' encouraged Marvin. 'Focus on him. Try to picture him.'

What man? wondered Matty. Lucy hadn't

mentioned any man.

'It's no good,' said Lucy, opening her eyes. 'Nothing's happening.'

'Patience, grasshopper,' said Marvin. 'Rome wasn't built in a day.'

Lucy glared at him.

'Try thinking about why you might have come here,' continued Marvin, ignoring the look she had given him.

'Why I came here.' Lucy closed her eyes again. 'Or why I was brought here.'

Matty's own thoughts drifted to that possibility. Had Lucy been kidnapped and forced into the past? Or was she running away from something? Perhaps that strange woman who had been following them had something to do with it? An image of her formed in his mind. It distorted and melted away as other images forced their way forward. An explosion. Injured people. People dying. Screaming people. People running. Fleeing. A fear gripped his insides and squeezed the breath out of him. Someone was after him. Someone who meant him harm.

'Aaarggghh!' A stabbing pain seared through his head. It felt like his eyes were about to pop and his brain explode.

His eyes had snapped shut with the pain, but Matty now tried to force them open. He managed to open them a tiny crack, his head still throbbing.

Everything was blurred and indistinct.

'Aaarggghh!' He heard his own scream repeated, even though his mouth remained clenched tight. And beyond that, another scream. Lucy's?

He breathed in deeply, held it and managed to get his eyes open all the way. Marvin's face swam into view. It was doubled, tripled, quadrupled, like a multiple exposure photo.

'Are…'

'Are…'

'Are…'

'…you…'

'…you…'

'…you…'

'…okay?'

'…okay?'

'…okay?'

The multiple Marvins were talking to him, blurring together and separating.

'Are you…'

'Are you…'

'Are you…'

'…okay?'

'…okay?'

'…okay?'

All the moving Marvins were making him nauseous. He closed his eyes to block them and realised he was still holding his breath.

He exhaled and then drew in a heaving gasp of air.

Another stab of pain drove through his mind, accompanied by a face. A boy's face. It was changing. Transforming. Morphing and aging. And then it was splitting apart, leaves forcing themselves out from under the skin. Flowers budding and bursting. Until there was nothing but vegetation. A heaving, suffocating mass of greenery.

The pain crescendoed.

And Matty was swallowed by darkness.

Matty's head hurt. It was just a dull ache in the darkness now. He opened his eyes.

Marvin's face swam into view. There was just one of him this time. And then Lucy's face joined in, all creased with concern.

'You okay?' she asked.

'Yeah,' he croaked in response, turning his head slowly from one side to the other. He was lying on the floor behind the Space/Time Books table, Marvin and Lucy on their knees beside him.

'Had us worried there for a bit,' said Marvin.

'Couple of the people here wanted to call an ambulance when you passed out,' said Lucy.

'Did anything happen?' asked Matty.

'Yeah!' Lucy's voice was full of excitement. 'That repeating time thing happened again. Only much more.'

'I experienced it too,' added Marvin, his face not giving anything away. 'Not to the same extent as Lucy, but enough to confirm that something screwy is happening with time. And a few other people in here also must have felt something, because they were confused for a few seconds. Rubbing their eyes and shaking their heads.' Slowly, his eyes widened. 'Like wow!' Then he burst into a grin. 'It was super amazing!' He was now literally bouncing around in front of Matty. 'Do you realise what this means? Huh? Do ya? Do ya?' He didn't wait for Matty to answer. 'Everything has changed. I literally mean... ev-er-y-thing! The boundaries of human knowledge have been extended. The universe has expanded.'

'Time travel is real,' whispered Matty, still lying on the floor. Despite everything that had happened, despite him bringing Lucy to ask Marvin about time travel, in the back of his mind, if he was really honest with himself, he had still doubted it. But now it was confirmed. 'Time travel is real.'

'Yeah, yeah, yeah!' Marvin continued to bounce around in front of him.

Matty began to tremble, a shiver that started in his toes and worked its way up his whole body.

'But... that... means...' He could barely form the words.

'Yeah, yeah, yeah!'

'And that…'

'Yeah, yeah, yeah!'

'Which means…'

'Yeah, yeah, yeah!'

'All those books…'

'Yeah, yeah, yeah!'

'And movies…'

'Yeah, yeah, yeah!'

'And there might be…'

'Yeah, yeah, yeah!'

'Time travellers all over the place.' Matty finally managed a coherent string of words.

'And we just don't know about it.' Marvin waved his arms about. 'Anyone here might be a time traveller and we just don't know it.'

'That's… that's…' Matty had lost his words again.

'Exciting!' finished Marvin.

'Yeah,' agreed Matty.

'Yeah, yeah, yeah!'

'Can you two tone it down a notch?' asked Lucy.

'Sure.' Marvin reined it in instantaneously, eyes returning to their normal width, stupid grin reducing to a slight smirk.

'Cool.' Matty sat up and then groaned. 'I feel terrible.'

'So,' said Lucy, 'I guess all this makes me a confirmed time traveller.'

'Yeahhhhhhh…' Marvin became suddenly

serious. 'About that. If Lucy is the time traveller, why is Matty being so strongly affected by this?'

'We figured that we must be connected in some way,' said Lucy. 'Maybe because he was the first person I met after arriving.'

'That's all well and good,' said Marvin, looking at Lucy. 'But Matty's reaction was worse than yours. You didn't pass out and drop like a stone to the floor.'

'Maybe he's just sensitive.' Lucy smirked. 'Not as strong as me.'

'Maybe.' Marvin got to his feet and extended a hand to Matty, helping him up. 'But I'm not convinced.'

'Now what do we do?' asked Matty.

'Get down,' ordered Lucy, pushing him back onto the floor behind the table.

'What? Why?'

'That woman's here,' said Lucy. 'The one that's been following us.'

'Someone's been following you?' asked Marvin. 'Why didn't you tell me?'

'I dunno,' said Matty. 'Didn't seem as important as all the other stuff.' He peered up over the edge of the table. 'Where is she?'

'By the door,' hissed Lucy.

'Which one is she?' asked Marvin.

'Grey coat. White hair. Sunglasses.'

'Got her,' said Marvin. 'The one that looks like a

Fed.'

'Why are we hiding?' asked Matty, trying to peek out from behind the Space/Time Books sign that hung down the front of the table. 'Last time she showed up we chased her.'

'Yeah, and she got away by using some sort of time distortion.'

'What?' Marvin practically shouted his disbelief. 'When were you planning on telling me about this?'

'Sorry,' said Lucy. 'Asking you to believe that I travelled through time was a big enough ask without adding her into the mix.'

'What should we do?' asked Matty, giving up on trying to see around the sign. Part of him wanted to confront her. But part of him just wanted to run away. He looked to Lucy to make the decision.

'Let's follow her and see what she gets up to,' suggested Lucy. 'Marvin, what's she doing now?'

'She's looking around. Now she's looking down as her wrist. She's got some sort of weird bracelet or something. She's sort of fiddling with it. And… and now she holding her wrist up and kind of pointing it around the room.' He paused. 'Hang on. She's coming this way.'

'Keep her busy,' ordered Lucy. Then to Matty: 'Follow me.'

She crawled off to the next table, concealed by the banner signage, making a shushing sign with a finger to her lips when the stallholder looked down at her with surprise, and then on to the next. Matty followed, smiling apologetically at the stallholders as he went. Making it to the far table, they slipped out from under it and took refuge behind a large potted plant, its leaves brown and drooping.

Matty reached out and touched one of the leaves. It crumbled beneath his fingers. 'The plant is dead.'

'Who cares,' said Lucy, peering out from behind it, back towards Space/Time Books.

The woman was gesticulating wildly, while Marvin scratched his head and shrugged. It seemed like he was doing a fine job of playing dumb, much to the woman's frustration. She leaned forward across the table as if about to grab Marvin, when she seemed to think better of it. Instead, she crouched down, lifted the sign and checked under the table. Marvin protested, but she just gave him a rude gesture and moved on to the next table. She didn't bother speaking to the stallholder and just checked under his table without a word of explanation.

'She'll get to us eventually,' said Matty. 'What do we do?'

'Next time she crouches down,' said Lucy, 'we make a break for the door.'

Matty glanced towards the door. 'Look!' A man and woman in military uniform marched into the room. Were they people in costume? Lots of science fiction had military characters, after all. Approaching the nearest table, they started questioning the stallholder, moving along to the next when they were done. *Perhaps they really were soldiers,* he thought, as he remembered the military vehicle at the shops yesterday. They certainly had an air of authority about them.

Lucy tapped Matty on the shoulder and indicated the woman in grey. She was no longer searching for them and was eyeing the soldiers furtively. Then she made a beeline for the door.

'Come on,' said Lucy, also heading for the door. 'Let's follow her.'

'But I've left my backpack under the table.'

'You can get it later,' said Lucy, jumping to her feet.

They raced out the door and slammed straight into the woman, who appeared to have been waiting for them.

'I knew you were in there,' she said, her voice a mixture of annoyance and relief. 'You need to come with me. Now!'

Lucy turned to Matty. 'RUN!'

LUCY

– CHAPTER ELEVEN –

ARRIVAL

'No! Wait! Stop.'

Lucy heard the woman calling from behind as they raced down the corridor.

'There!' Matty pointed to the fire escape door up ahead.

Lucy followed him into the concrete stairwell and down the steps. As they reached the ground floor they heard the door above them opening and the woman yelling again.

'You are in danger!'

Lucy stopped, hand on the exit door. Danger? She peered up the stairwell to see the woman leaning over the railing, just in time to see the sunglasses slip from her face. The woman grabbed at them but they fell over the railing. Lucy thought she saw a flash of green light from the woman's eyes before she pulled back out of sight.

The sunglasses smashed onto the concrete by

Lucy's feet.

'Did you just see…' Matty voice trailed away.

'Yep.'

Lucy shouldered open the door and the two of them ran out into the foyer. It was immediately obvious that something was wrong. People were clustered around the entrance, looking out into the street through the windows. Lucy could hear the sound of muffled sirens.

Was it connected to them? wondered Lucy. It felt like something important was happening. She was determined to find out. Rushing towards the doors, she manoeuvred her way through the onlookers and out into the street, with Matty following along.

They were just in time to see a police car, light flashing, siren blaring, streak past.

Lucy followed it with her eyes, as it weaved through oncoming traffic to turn into the street just half a block ahead of them. The sign read 'Little Collins Street'.

'Come on.' Convinced that this was somehow all connected, Lucy raced up to the corner.

About a block down Little Collins Street, just ahead of the next intersection, the police car slowed down to join more flashing lights. The siren cut out. There was a crowd forming.

Without a word to each other, Lucy and Matty headed off at a jog. She felt drawn, like something was tugging at her – a need to find out what was happening. The police were moving people back and setting up a boundary of orange traffic cones as they arrived.

Lucy jumped up and down trying to see over the crowd of people, catching glimpses of bright light.

'Please move back,' announced a police officer using a megaphone. 'This situation may be dangerous. For your own safety, please stand back.'

As people began to back off, Lucy took Matty's hand and together they squeezed forward through the crowd, until they could finally see what all the excitement was about.

There was a sphere of… something. Energy? A ball of energy? Hovering just above the pavement, it sizzled and sparked and glowed, contracting and expanding, shifting from basketball size to roughly the width of a small car. As its dimensions reduced, one of the policemen, gun drawn and pointed shakily ahead of him, tentatively approached. He was almost within reach when it flared. And then he was back where he started, approaching again, one hesitant step at a time.

'Did you see that?' asked Matty, voice barely a whisper.

'Yep,' answered Lucy. 'But no one else seems to have.'

And then it happened again. The policeman

reached the sphere. It flared, the intensity greater this time. Everyone about Lucy and Matty shifted with a nauseating skip in time.

'Please move back. This situation may be dangerous. For you own safety, please stand back.'

The policeman was speaking through his megaphone again, the people shuffling back.

'Distortions in time,' said Matty.

'Another time traveller?' suggested Lucy.

A squeal of tyres announced the arrival of several military vehicles as they came careening around the corner beyond the crowd. Two jeeps and a troop van screeched to a halt and armed soldiers disembarked.

The police seemed taken aback, and a number of the gathered crowd started to break away.

'Everyone please stay calm and remain where you are,' shouted the soldier who appeared to be in charge.

Lucy's attention was drawn back to the sphere as it sizzled and sparked and grew larger. It flared again. Brighter. So intense that everyone lifted hands and arms to shield their eyes.

Reality blurred and skipped and stuttered around Lucy and Matty, as people and vehicles faded away. Lucy realised she was still holding Matty's hand, the two of them alone in being unaffected by the distortion.

And then everything settled.

The soldiers and their vehicles were gone.

The police were no longer there.

There were no people gathered.

It was just Lucy and Matty, standing on the pavement staring at the spot where the energy sphere had been. It wasn't there anymore. Instead, there was a mass of writhing green tentacles. No, not tentacles... vines. As Lucy watched in dumbfounded silence, the vines began to wither and brown. As they fell away and disintegrated, they revealed a person. Short and slight, their features seemed unstable. They were young and old at the same time. Their clothes were also indistinct – a shimmering sort of all-covering green. Were they clothes at all?

And then the figure became distinct – a boy in green. Lucy thought he was about ten at most. But then he changed, his features morphing, his body growing taller and broader. He was a young man now. And then a not-so-young man. And then middle-aged. And then a young man again. Back and forth, his features and apparent age fluctuated. Finally, he settled down. He was a boy again – sixteen, maybe seventeen. His eyes flashed an eerie green in his expressionless face.

'What just happened?' asked Matty.

'Beats me!'

Matty began to back away. 'He doesn't seem

friendly, does he?'

'No. No he doesn't.'

The boy took a faltering step forward, as if he were only just learning how to use his legs. Passersby ignored him, continuing on their way as if he wasn't there. He took another step, and another, gaining purpose with each.

'I've got a bad feeling about this,' said Matty.

'Me too.' Lucy turned to see the woman in grey approaching from the direction of the hotel. 'Uh-oh!'

'What do we do?' asked Matty.

'I don't know.'

A squeal of tyres announced the arrival of several military vehicles as they came careening around the corner. Two jeeps and a troop van screeched to a halt and armed soldiers disembarked.

The soldier who had spoken to the crowd of people last time around was now barking orders at his troops. Seconds later they had the boy surrounded. Passerby slowed to watch, but one of the soldiers waved them on.

Glancing over her shoulder, Lucy checked to see what the woman in grey was up to. But she was nowhere to be seen. As Lucy returned her attention to the green boy and the soldiers, time did a hop, skip and jump. People stopped, actions repeated, movements slowed and sped up…

And the boy was gone.

The soldiers that had been surrounding him were looking about in confusion. The one in charge marched up to join them, issuing orders as he went. Then all eyes were on Lucy and Matty.

'They're staring at us,' said Lucy.

The officer pointed at them.

Matty turned to Lucy. 'RUN!'

'We seem to be doing an awful lot of running,' said Lucy, as they ran up Little Collins Street. 'Where are we going?' she cried.

'Back to the hotel. And the convention. Lots of people there. Lots of places to hide.'

'Right!'

Lucy and Matty were still holding hands. But Lucy was running faster and her fingers finally slipped away as they rounded the corner back onto Exhibition Street. As they slowed their approach to go through the hotel doors, she looked back to see four soldiers appearing at the corner.

In the foyer, the first thing Lucy noticed was that no one was gathered around the entrance. The time distortion had obviously reached at least this far.

Lucy made for the fire escape stairs and Matty followed.

'Should we go back to Marvin?' Matty asked as they raced up the steps.

'No. Too open. We need to find someplace to hide.'

They continued up. As they were passing the fourth floor entrance, the door flew open. The woman in grey was standing there, cracked sunglasses slightly askew on her face. Lucy almost laughed.

'Please don't run away,' the woman pleaded. 'You're in danger and I'm trying to help. Please, come with me.'

Lucy saw the indecision on Matty's face. 'Better than soldiers,' she suggested, tentatively.

Below, they heard the door from the foyer burst open and the sound of booted feet on steps.

Matty nodded reluctantly and the two of them went through, the woman closing the door quietly behind them. This floor was all accommodation and she led them straight to the first room. She pressed her wrist up against the door and Lucy caught a glimpse of something green and sinewy wrapped around it as the door sprang open.

'Is this your room?' asked Lucy, as they entered.

'No.' The woman strode across the space and drew the curtains.

It was an ordinary hotel room, with one double bed, a couch, a desk and a chair. There wasn't any luggage lying around and the bed was made, so it seemed that it was unoccupied.

'Why have I lost my memory? How did I get here?' demanded Lucy, confronting the woman.

'What?' The woman glared at her from behind her broken glasses. 'I didn't bring you. I have no idea who you are or why you're here. I just had to make sure you weren't a threat.' She took a deep breath. 'But it seems that the real threat has now arrived and so it's my duty to deal with it.'

'Huh?' Lucy was confused. 'But I thought…'

'Well, you thought wrong.' The woman lifted her hand to her face and Lucy caught another glimpse of green beneath the cuff of her coat. 'I have located the prince,' she said, seemingly speaking into whatever it was that encircled her wrist. 'Dispatch the pod.' The woman turned to face Matty. 'It's you I'm here to protect, Your Highness.'

MATTY

– CHAPTER TWELVE –

PRINCE FROM THE FUTURE

'What? Me?' Matty stared at the woman in disbelief. Why would he need protecting? He opened his mouth to speak and then closed it again. Wait! Highness? 'I... but... well...' He paused to try to get his thoughts in order. He pointed to Lucy. 'But she's the time traveller.'

'Yes, she has travelled in time. She is giving off enough residual artron energy to surmise that she has travelled through time more than once.'

'More than once...' echoed Lucy.

'But you, Matty, have also travelled in time.'

'Me? But she's the one causing these weird time disturbances.'

'No!' The woman was quite emphatic. 'That is definitely you. Or, more precisely, a combination of you and your would-be assassin.'

'Assassin?' It was little more than a hoarse

whisper. Matty's throat had gone dry. He swallowed as he tried to take in this new information. An assassin? Someone was trying to kill him? Was it that strange boy out on the city street?

'Wait... what?' Lucy's face was white, her eyes wide. 'You don't mean me, do you?'

The woman sighed. 'There's a lot you don't know. And a lot that's happening. Why don't you both sit down and I'll try to explain.'

Matty barely heard the woman. His mind was still focused on the whole assassination thing. A vague memory came to the surface – him being scared for his life as others around him died. He sat on the edge of the bed next to Lucy, although far enough away from her to make a break for it, just in case.

'My name is Ashna,' said the woman, her voice much more gentle than before. She took her sunglasses off, sighed as she inspected the crack, then tossed them onto the desk. Matty was pleased to see that her eyes, although a vibrant green, were not glowing. Perhaps they had imagined that in the stairwell.

'Things are a bit critical at the moment and we don't have much time. So I'll try to explain as quickly and as clearly as I can.' She nodded at Matty and Lucy before continuing. 'Matthew, your real name is Jaria Dawn Thrice, Crown Prince of the Aslante

Separation, and you are from fifty thousand years in the future.'

'Fifty thousand years.' Matty was still speaking in a disbelieving whisper, his mind dazed by what he was hearing.

'So,' said Lucy. 'Am I from then as well?'

'No,' replied Ashna. 'I'm not sure what time period you are from, but it is far more recent. Although as I mentioned before, the residual artron energy indicates multiple time travels. It is that, as well as your unknown origin, that initially concerned me. I was investigating you to determine whether or not you were a threat.'

'Which I'm not,' asserted Lucy.

'I'm beginning to think that, but you have certainly endangered the prince.'

'What's that supposed to mean?'

'Your presence has caused some of the prince's memories to resurface. Although small and indistinct they have, nevertheless, caused psychic ripples. Ripples which have been observed by his enemies, allowing them to track him and send an assassin.'

Matty looked at Lucy. 'So you're not the only one with amnesia.'

Lucy gave him a wan smile. 'Hooray!'

'Your memories were deliberately suppressed,' explained Ashna, 'for your own safety. As for Lucy,

I can only guess that for some reason the travel caused a form of trauma.'

'Great,' said Lucy, giving Matty a playful punch on the arm. 'You were right. Brain damage.'

'While our people possess time travel, it is not precise.' Ashna continued with her explanation. 'And given that we were trying to hide you, not being able to pinpoint your exact destination was a good thing. But our enemies procured a thought-scan from the royal archives, giving them the ability to track you. So the decision was made to repress your memories and implant a false identity.'

'So I'm not really me...' This made Matty feel suddenly sad. He thought that he should, perhaps, be outraged or annoyed or something like that. But he just felt sad. Sad that his interests, likes and experiences were not real. That he was a fake person. And then it suddenly occurred to him: if he was a fake person, what about his parents? Were they fake too?

'We did have your permission,' Ashna assured him. 'You were not happy about it, but you understood the necessity.'

'Maybe I did. Maybe I didn't,' said Matty. 'But that doesn't make any of this easier now.'

'I know.' Ashna's gaze softened as she regarded him. 'And I am sorry. I am also sorry that we have reached our current crisis point.' She sighed and her eyes hardened a little, taking on a more determined air. 'There is more to tell you.' She paused as if trying to determine just where to start.

'So,' said Matty. 'Will I now get my real memories back? Will this me, Matthew, Matty, just fade away?' He felt his sadness begin to morph into fear. Fear that he would lose everything that he thought he was.

'No. I do not have the capacity to do this now. It will have to wait until we return to our own time. Which we cannot do until the retrieval pod arrives. As I have already said, travelling back in time is imprecise. While our people have my thought scan to home in on, it will still be… inexact. So I need to keep you safe until the pod arrives—'

'You keep going on about your people,' Lucy interrupted. 'And about your enemies. So… who… what…'

Ashna placed her hands behind her back, as if about to begin a lecture to a room full of students. 'The political situation in the future was rather unstable, to say the least. For safety the prince was hidden in the past, with the intention of retrieving him when the time was opportune. We did not bank on our enemies locating him and sending an assassin. This now complicates matters.'

'Woah!' Lucy shook her head. 'I'm finding this hard to take in.'

'Imagine how I feel,' said Matty. 'Hard to take in' was an understatement. He felt like his brain was about to explode.

'What was that?' demanded Ashna, suddenly turning to the door.

'What was what?' asked Lucy.

'I thought I heard—'

The door burst open and soldiers came rushing in.

LUCY

– CHAPTER THIRTEEN –

GRANDAD

What's going on? thought Lucy, as the green-uniformed people came barraging into the hotel room. She jumped to her feet, only to have a tall female soldier put a restraining hand on her shoulder.

Another soldier approached Matty.

Before Ashna could do anything, the final two soldiers had her arms held behind her. 'Let go of me!' she demanded.

'You can't do this,' said Lucy.

'Actually, we can,' said the female soldier beside her.

'You sound like a pom,' said Matty's soldier.

'So what!' Lucy was desperately trying to sound brave and defiant but wasn't so sure she was succeeding.

'So we'll need to see your passport.'

'Plenty of time for ID later,' said Lucy's soldier. 'For now, let's report in and take them downstairs.'

'Roger that!' Matty's soldier unclipped a radio from his belt and spoke into it. 'Joey 1 to Kanga. Joey 1 to Kanga. Witnesses apprehended. Over.'

'Joey 1, this is Kanga. Good work,' a brusque female voice crackled through the speaker. 'Bring them down via the service elevator. Less chance of causing a scene that way. We'll have a van waiting at the rear of the hotel. You're authorised to sedate them if necessary. Over and out.'

Lucy didn't like the sound of that. *Sedate them if necessary.* She also glanced nervously at the holster on her soldier's belt. None of them had gone for a weapon... yet.

'It won't be necessary, will it?' Lucy's soldier raised an eyebrow at her pointedly. Lucy shook her head. Matty did the same as she looked towards him. 'And you, miss?' she asked, looking finally to Ashna.

For a moment, Lucy thought Ashna was going to cause trouble, but eventually she sighed and said, 'Very well.'

With practiced efficiency, Lucy, Matty and Ashna were ushered from the room and quickly escorted down to the waiting van. Lucy and Matty's soldiers stayed with them in the back while the other two went up front.

'Who are you people?' asked Matty, as the van started moving. 'You're not ordinary soldiers.'

The windows in the back had been blacked out

and Lucy couldn't see where the van was going, so instead she watched the female soldier. She seemed to be the one in charge. And it was she who answered Matty.

'What makes you say that, young man?'

He pointed at her beret.

'Well spotted.'

Lucy studied the logo on the green fabric. It was circular. With letters. And it looked familiar.

'UNIT?' she whispered.

'Correct!' The soldier looked at her now, studying closely.

And suddenly, there in the back of the van where they were being held prisoner, it all came flooding back. Every. Single. Memory. Triggered by the logo. Triggered by the letters U.N.I.T., and all that they stood for. Her heart pounded with the joy of it. Her breath quickened as she ran through her memories with elation. Her life. Her school. Her friends. Her family. Her time ring. She glanced down at the ring on her finger and touched it lightly.

'An acronym?' asked Matty. 'What do the letters stand for?'

Lucy's mind was buzzing with all her returned memories. Absent for so long, they now all seemed to be fighting for prominence in her thoughts. But then the one that stood out, the one that was important now, suddenly filled her consciousness. It was the memory of her as a little girl, sitting on her grandad's knee, listening to his stories. His stories about...

'United Nations In—' began the soldier.

'Intelligence Taskforce,' finished Lucy.

'How do you know that?' asked Matty and the soldier in unison.

Memories of her grandfather filled Lucy's mind and her heart. How could she have forgotten him? A smile played at the corners of her mouth as she answered the question.

'Brigadier Alistair Gordon Lethbridge-Stewart is my grandfather.'

'Wait here!'

The soldier closed the door and Lucy could hear the click of the lock. She, Matty and Ashna were left in a small, office-like room, containing two plastic chairs, a filing cabinet and an old desk.

Lucy headed straight for the window. With the blacked-out glass in the van, she hadn't been able to see where they had been taken. She gazed down into what looked like the grounds of a factory, surrounded by high, electrified fences, beyond which were more factories and warehouses. They were on the second floor of a building.

She wished that Hobo was with her. He was her best friend and invaluable when they were off on an adventure. He wouldn't have let blacked out windows stop him from figuring out where they had gone. He would have mentally made note of every turn the vehicle took, and timed the trip and somehow worked it all out from that. She had a sudden realisation. What had happened to Hobo? She had travelled to the past with him. Did he make it back home?

'Exactly thirty-eight minutes,' said Matty.

'What?' Lucy turned away from the window to face him.

Matty tapped his digital watch. 'Travel time in the van. There was also a lot of stopping and starting during the journey. So probably heavy traffic. Which means we're not that far out from the city.' He walked over to the window and peered out. 'Yeah, look. You can see the city buildings in the distance. Looks like we're in the western industrial area.'

Lucy marvelled at Matty. Despite being dumped with all the stuff about being a prince from the future with false memories, targeted by an assassin, here he was, still obsessed with his digital watch. And using it to provide them with important information. She thought that was pretty cool! Actually, she realised, it was a bit Hobo-like. That made her feel comforted.

'An excellent place to conceal a secret paramilitary group,' observed Ashna, with what seemed like a grudging respect.

'Have you got your memories back then?' asked Matty, turning away from the window.

The drive from the city had become stony silent after Lucy's revelation. Matty had attempted to ask her about her memories then, but the soldier had told them all to be silent for the remainder of the journey. Now Matty finally had his chance.

'Yes,' Lucy replied, 'it was a sudden info dump of everything I had forgotten.'

'Hmmm,' said Ashna. 'Something must have triggered it.'

Lucy nodded. 'The UNIT logo. When I saw it, I knew what the letters stood for. And then I remembered my grandfather, who had told me all about UNIT. And then I remembered everything else.' She paused to get her thoughts straight. 'Bang! Just like that. Everything was back.' She still couldn't quite believe it. But it felt so good.

'So, why did the soldier get all weird about it?' asked Matty. 'She seemed pretty chatty before you said that name.'

'Ah well. The thing is, this is 1985.' She had, of course, realised her mistake the moment she had said it. 'You see, that's twenty-odd years before I was born. So my grandfather wasn't my grandfather yet. In fact, right now, he doesn't even know he has a son. He doesn't find out about my dad for a while yet. So… they probably think I'm lying. And they're probably wondering how I know about Brigadier Lethbridge-Stewart in the first place.'

Ashna huffed.

'What?' asked Lucy.

'You can't tell them about the future,' said Ashna. 'It's dangerous!'

'*You* told me about the future.'

'You are a time traveller. You are part of this. But the people here in this time, they need to be protected.'

'But UNIT know about time travel,' persisted Lucy. 'My grandfather told me about them.'

'It's best not to take chances.' Ashna paused, frowning in thought. 'But given the situation we are in, having been captured by them, and given that you have already given them some information, I think we can at least tell them the basics. But nothing more than we have to. And to as few people as possible.'

Lucy resented being told what to do by this person. *Is she a defender of Earth? Or a Child of January? Has she travelled in time with HG Wells?* she thought. Lucy understood time travel all too well because of her many adventures and Lethbridge-Stewart blood coursing through her veins.

'It sounds sensible,' said Matty, looking at Lucy with a hopeful expression.

'Okay, okay,' agreed Lucy. She wandered over to the desk and sullenly examined the items sitting there – a desk lamp, some stationary and a Tupperware container. She opened the container to find sandwiches. They looked stale, with wilted lettuce spilling out from the sides. It made her realise just how hungry she was, but the sandwiches were so unappetising she closed the lid back on them.

'Right,' said Ashna. 'Now that's settled, we need to work out how we're going to deal with this.'

The sound of the door unlocking made them all turn. A short, uniformed woman entered. She was obviously someone of rank, as she wore a jacket covered in stripes, insignia and ribbons, and a hat rather than a beret. Lucy was surprised at just how short she was, for someone who appeared to be middle-aged. She was no taller than Lucy herself, which wasn't very tall at all. Despite her size she had the bearing of authority, perfect posture and a steely glint in her eyes.

'Wait outside,' she instructed the soldier who had opened the door for her. The man saluted and left.

Lucy thought she might have been the voice they'd heard over the soldier's radio – the one that had said, 'You're authorised to sedate them if necessary.'

'Lieutenant Colonel Hardy,' announced the woman, as she now surveyed the occupants of the room. 'And you would be?'

'Ashna.'

'Ah, well, Matthew Franklin, I guess.'

'Lucy Wilson.'

'Hmm.' The lieutenant colonel placed her hands behind her back and rocked forward onto the balls of her feet. 'What an interesting group. Someone with only one name. Someone who seems uncertain of their name. And someone claiming to be related to Brigadier Lethbridge-Stewart.' Her eyes came to rest upon Lucy. 'I've known Alistair for a number of years and he's never mentioned a granddaughter. And, if you will forgive me, you appear to be of the wrong…' She paused, obviously choosing her next word carefully. '… ethnicity.'

And there it is, thought Lucy. She sighed. It was 1985, she reminded herself.

'I get my skin colour from my mum's side of the family,' Lucy declared. 'My dad is the Brigadier's son, although Grandad doesn't know it yet.'

'I beg your pardon.' Lieutenant Colonel Hardy was now staring at Lucy as if she were quite mad.

Ashna groaned and Lucy caught her scowl of disapproval.

'But… ah…' Lucy stumbled on. 'I'm from the future so you shouldn't tell Grandad about me.'

'Brigadier Lethbridge-Stewart is currently in Geneva and unavailable,' said Hardy. 'So even if I wanted to tell him, I couldn't.' She cleared her throat. 'More importantly, you're now claiming to be a time traveller. Given what happened in the Melbourne

CBD earlier, I—'

'Excuse me,' interrupted Ashna. 'Before this gets out of hand, I think it would be better if I explained things.'

'Oh, please do.' Hardy waved a hand at her. 'I'm dying to know what's going on.'

Lucy was slightly resentful of Ashna taking over, but, truth be told, also a bit relieved. She wasn't sure how to explain everything.

'All three of us are from the future,' Ashna declared.

Lucy watched Hardy's eyebrows gain altitude as Ashna began her explanations.

'In order to protect the timeline and not cause any unnecessary anomalies, it would be best that we only give you the information you really need.'

'How thoughtful.' The lieutenant colonel's voice was oozing sarcasm as she glared at the woman.

'Our origins are not important,' continued Ashna, unperturbed by Hardy's attitude. 'What is important is that an assassin from the future arrived here in Melbourne earlier today. I believe your soldiers witnessed the event, although how much they remember of it is anyone's guess. There has been a significant amount of localised time manipulation. The crux of the matter, however, is that this assassin is here to kill the Cr…' She paused to correct herself. 'Matthew. It is imperative that he be kept secure until we are able to return to our own time.'

'I see.' The lieutenant colonel rolled forward onto the balls of her feet again, and this time up onto her toes, as if trying to make herself taller; then back down. 'And I assume you can prove all of this.'

Ashna opened her mouth to reply, but then grimaced in pain and clutched her right arm. Then with a scream she thrust her arm towards Matty and lunged at him.

Lucy watched with wide eyes as Ashna's hand stopped inches from Matty's face, her fingers stretching towards him. But she appeared to be resisting. Her left hand grasped her right arm and tried to hold it back.

'What are you doing?' asked Matty.

'I'm trying… to stop… myself from killing you.' Ashna's voice was strained as she fought against some unseen force.

'Your wrist,' gasped Matty, staring at the coil of green that circled around it.

Ashna's bracelet was unravelling, sinewy little plant-like vines unwrapping and reaching out towards him.

Matty's face betrayed his shock as he backed away. Ashna followed, as if being pulled by her own arm until she had Matty pressed up against the wall.

MATTY

– CHAPTER FOURTEEN –

INVASION OF THE TIME TRAVELLING PLANT PEOPLE

Hardy banged on the door. 'Private, get in here.' The green tendrils reached out again and gently brushed Matty's face. It was strangely soothing. He could feel his muscles start to relax and his fear ebb away. From the corner of his eye he saw the door open, the soldier walk in and stand bemusedly gaping at the scene that was unfolding. *It's okay,* thought Matty. *I feel fine.*

Ashna grunted with effort and managed to take a step back, pulling the tendrils away from Matty. The sinewy green vines waved about as if trying to re-establish contact with him, then a flower bud began to grow from the end of one.

'No!' screamed Ashna, as she reached out with her free hand and grabbed the bud, yanking it from the vine.

The tendrils flailed about in distress as Ashna crushed the bud in her fist. Then they turned on her, pulling her own hand to her throat.

'Help me!' she demanded, as she started to choke herself.

The soldier ran forward, uncertainly gripping Ashna's attacking arm and trying to twist it up behind her. As he did so, the vines slipped from her wrist onto the floor.

'Look!' shouted Lucy, pointing at the disengaged plant.

It was still moving, squirming towards Matty. And Matty, feeling slightly dazed, found himself reaching out towards it.

'Stay away from it!' called Lucy, darting forward to take hold of him.

The plant coiled itself up like a spring and launched into the air at them, but Lucy managed to pull Matty out of the way. The tendrils hit the wall and clung, swaying from side to side.

'Let go of me,' demanded Ashna, as the soldier continued to hold her arm twisted behind her back.

Hardy stepped forward drawing her pistol and aiming at the plant.

'Wait,' said Lucy, dashing to the desk and snatching up the Tupperware container. Discarded sandwiches spilled onto the floor as she wrenched the lid off and lunged for the wall, just as the tendril sprang towards Matty again. She intercepted the plant in mid-air with the container, slamming the lid onto it, and sealing in the possessed plant.

The container jumped about in her hands alarmingly and she quickly placed it on the floor, stepping away.

'You can always count on Tupperware to seal in the freshness,' she joked, but no one took any notice.

The container jumped and rattled about on the floor for a few more seconds before becoming still.

'What the hell just happened?' demanded the lieutenant colonel, holstering her pistol, eyes glued to the container on the floor.

'Just the first assassination attempt,' gasped Ashna, who was still being restrained by the soldier. 'Now would you please let me go?'

Hardy nodded and the soldier released her.

'Explain!' demanded Hardy.

'The assassin,' said Ashna through gritted teeth, as she massaged her shoulder, 'took control of my chloro-sym.'

'For heaven's sake, woman, would you speak plain English?' blustered Hardy.

'A chloro-sym is a plant-based interface. It allows me to access an information database as well as manipulate things physically.'

'That's what you used to open the hotel room

door,' said Lucy.

'I have a telepathic link with it,' continued Ashna, ignoring Lucy. 'No one else should be able to control it. And yet...'

Matty slumped into one of the chairs. He felt drained. The calmness instilled by the tendrils had dissipated. Everything had suddenly become very real. His life was in danger! 'What do we do?'

Ashna straightened up. 'What we do now is keep you safe.'

'Private Larkins,' barked Hardy, 'you will remain here to guard our guests and the contents of this box.' She turned to the others. 'I'll put the base on high alert and get our science advisor down here to collect the specimen. If you will please wait here for the moment, I'll have you escorted to a high security area shortly. I'll then expect a full briefing on just what the hell is going on here.' She rolled onto her toes again and glared at Ashna. 'If you withhold any information, any information at all, then you will be treated as hostile and will be locked up. Do I make myself clear?'

'Perfectly,' muttered Ashna.

Hardy executed a precision turn on her heel and left the room.

'How did the assassin do all that?' asked Lucy, once Hardy had gone.

Ashna glanced at Private Larkins, who had

stationed himself by the door.

Lucy rolled her eyes. 'Given everything that's happened, do we really need to be worried about how much the UNIT people know?'

'And it's my life in danger,' added Matty. 'If there's going to be another attempt made to bump me off, I'd like as much information as possible, so that, you know, I might be able to avoid it.'

'Very well.' Ashna nodded slowly, keeping her voice low. 'I fear that the assassin has had heavy genetic enhancement. In order to control my chloro-sym like that, he certainly has more than me.'

'You?' asked Lucy.

'Yes, I've been genetically enhanced using plant matter. As have all the people of the Aslante Separation.'

'What?' Matty felt the blood drain from his face. 'But... does that mean...' He couldn't bring himself to finish asking.

'Yes,' answered Ashna. 'You are.'

'I'm a plant person,' whispered Matty. He felt like his brain was about to explode with this latest revelation. He couldn't help but think about the sci-fi books and films with plant people. They never ended well. 'Just like...' he muttered. '*Invasion of the Body Snatchers*.'

'I have no idea what that is,' said Ashna.

'It's a film,' explained Lucy, her voice slow and

deliberate. 'Hobo loves it. Alien plants invade Earth and take people over. They become plant people. No longer human.'

'I can assure you that the prince is very much a human being.' She sighed. 'However… it is this perception that he and others like him must somehow be less than human, that led to the Aslante Separation in the first place. But that is history.' She gave Matty a wan smile. 'Albeit future history given that we're currently in 1985.'

'Is there any other future history we need to know?' asked Lucy.

'Just that the prince became a pawn in a power struggle. Which is why he was hidden in the past.'

'Yeah, well… that's kind of a lot to take in,' said Lucy.

'Imagine how I feel.' Matty was acutely aware of how shaky his voice was.

'Sorry.' Lucy lowered her eyes and an awkward silence descended.

Matty felt himself falling into another well of fearful thoughts, when Lucy spoke again.

'Just how much genetic plant enhancement have you had?'

Matty looked up to see her staring accusingly at Ashna.

'I'm a royal guardian. So, more than most.' Ashna's face was grave. 'The limit of what's considered safe.'

'What does that mean?' asked Matty.

'It means that we are at a disadvantage. As you have already seen, the assassin has greater abilities than me. But...' She paused. 'We may have an advantage in another way. Modifications such as mine come with risks, but mine are within acceptable risk parameters. This assassin has had extreme enhancement. He is at greater risk.'

'What sort of risk?' asked Lucy.

'That is hard to say,' admitted Ashna. 'I'm a guardian, not a geneticist.'

'When he arrived,' said Lucy, brow crinkling in thought, 'he kept changing. He looked really young at first. Then grew up and then got younger again.'

'An unstable personal timeline...' Ashna nodded thoughtfully. 'It could be. Especially if his modifications included an implanted time travel pod.'

Implanted time travel pod? When Ashna had first mentioned a retrieval pod, Matty had pictured a large metal thing, like an escape pod from a spaceship in a sci-fi book. Something big enough to comfortably seat a couple of people. Obviously he had been wrong. If it could be implanted, then it must be something small. Maybe it was organic? Like a seedpod? That would make sense.

Matty suddenly felt claustrophobic as thoughts

of genetic modification ran through his mind. How much had he been genetically altered? Did royalty have more enhancement than ordinary citizens? Were his modifications within the acceptable risk parameters Ashna had mentioned? He could feel his stomach churn and flip as his anxiety levels rose. He swallowed down the nausea and shuddered. Is this why he liked trees and flowers so much? Is this why he spent so much time out in the garden at home? He had a vision of himself turning into a plant – leaves and shoots and buds forcing their way through his skin. He shivered again.

He wandered over to the window, hoping the view would distract his thoughts. He could see a row of hedges below the window, running high along the wall of the building, and a few more scraggly ones out along the perimeter of the fence. His eyes caught movement.

'Um, guys, you might want to come and take a look at this.'

Lucy and Ashna came to join him, but Private Larkins stayed by the door, as impassive as he'd been throughout their conversation.

Matty pointed at a section of the fence to the right. A figure stood beyond the wire – all in green, head tilted up in their direction. Matty caught a flash of emerald from the figure's eyes, making him take a step back from the window.

'It's him,' said Ashna. She turned to the soldier. 'You might want to let your commander know the assassin is here.'

The soldier never had the chance to respond. The glass shattered and branches came smashing through the window, flinging Matty and Lucy to the ground and causing Ashna to stagger back. Private Larkins fired off a few ineffectual shots before the vegetation wrapped around him and yanked him through the window.

'What the…' began Lucy, springing to her feet.

'There are bushes along the wall below us,' explained Matty, also scrambling upright.

'So he can control the local vegetation too,' said Ashna. 'Making it grow and mutate. How annoying!'

More branches were now cascading into the room, wriggling their way towards Matty, Lucy and Ashna. They ran for the door.

'It's locked!' Ashna began banging on the door and shouting. 'We're being attacked! We need help!'

The branches snaked across the floor towards them, sprouting new leaves as they went. One of them wrapped itself around the Tupperware container, squeezing it, trying to release Ashna's chloro-sym.

'We've got to do something,' shouted Lucy, as Ashna continued to bang on the door.

Through the broken window they could hear

distant yelling, quickly followed by gunfire.

Matty's eyes searched the room, desperately hoping for something they could use as a weapon. He pointed to the filing cabinet. 'We could use that to block the window.'

Lucy gaped. 'I don't think it's big enough.'

'It's all we've got!'

Dodging branches, they dashed to the cabinet and started to push it towards the window.

'Aaargh!'

Matty saw the invading bush had wrapped a branch around Ashna's leg and was trying to pull her to the window. 'Tip it over,' he shouted at Lucy, as he began to rock the filing cabinet.

The two of them heaved the cabinet over, the draws spitting out files as it came crashing down onto the branches. At the same time the sound of more shouting could be heard from out in the grounds. With a final yank, the branch holding the Tupperware container removed the lid. Then the bush went limp, collapsing onto the floor. The leaves browned and fell off before their eyes. The branches dried and withered.

'Watch out!' gasped Ashna.

A green shoot was growing up out of the open container. Matty watched as a flower budded and bloomed from the tip. The petals opened and a spray of pollen puffed into the air. The little particles swirled around and then formed into a pattern, hanging in the middle of the room.

Matty's eyes were drawn to the motes dancing in the air before him. There was something strange about them. They weren't forming random patterns as he had first thought. They seemed to be coming together into symbols. Symbols that meant something.

'Danger?' he whispered, tentatively.

Behind them, the door banged open, and Lieutenant Colonel Hardy and two soldiers charged into the room. The pollen dissipated, the flower withered, and the chloro-sym shriveled and turned to dust.

'What the devil just happened?' demanded Hardy.

LUCY

– CHAPTER FIFTEEN –

MESSAGE

Lethbridge-Stewart stuff! That's what she and Hobo called all the weird and fantastical things they had faced. The sort of things that her grandad had dealt with when he was protecting Earth. That was what she was in the middle of – Lethbridge-Stewart stuff!

Although right at this moment, she appeared to be in a makeshift laboratory. The benches were covered in test tubes, Bunsen burners and other equipment. She, Matty and Ashna had been brought here by the lieutenant colonel and an armed escort. Deep in the centre of the building, the lab had no windows and was apparently a more easily guarded room for them to discuss things in.

After the three of them had finished telling Hardy about what had happened to them, the lieutenant colonel informed them that after bullets had failed, her troops had taken axes to the suddenly vicious vegetation in the grounds.

'Is this likely to continue?' asked Hardy. 'Plants coming to life and attacking my troops?'

'Plants are already alive,' Ashna pointed out.

'Don't be so damn pedantic,' snapped Hardy. 'You know what I mean.'

'Possibly,' conceded Ashna. 'So long as the assassin cannot get direct access to Matthew, control of local vegetation is his only option.'

'Right then.' Hardy rocked back and forth on her feet, the muscles in her face and neck taut. 'I'll see about getting some industrial strength weed-killer. In the meantime, we've got a couple of flamethrowers. That should help if there's another attack. But how do we deal with the assassin? And how do we find him?'

'You don't need to deal with him,' said Ashna. 'And you certainly don't need to find him. You just need to keep Matthew safe until our retrieval pod arrives and we can return to our own time. Once we are gone, he will also leave.'

'I'm afraid I can't take any chances,' said Hardy. 'What if this assassin doesn't leave after you're gone? What if your retrieval pod never arrives or, if it does, what if it doesn't work? What if an army of plants suddenly attacks my base and attempts to kill my troops? We need to have a backup.'

'Matthew is his only target,' explained Ashna.

'He will not kill anyone else, except myself and possibly Lucy, as we don't belong here.'

'We can't be sure of that.'

'Yes, you can. Time travel is a delicate business. There must be as little disruption as possible to the timeline. Any disruption is risky. Killing someone could be disastrous. It could adversely affect our future. The assassin knows this as well as I do. He will try to complete his mission in the same way I am trying to complete mine – with minimal impact. There will not be a full-on attack as that could put your troops in harm's way. The attacks so far have been via plant infiltration, directly focused on us.'

Lucy watched the exchange between the two women, glancing occasionally at Matty, wondering how he was coping with this rather matter-of-fact discussion about him being assassinated. She wasn't sure that she entirely believed Ashna. She had the feeling that this woman from the future was hiding something; keeping a vital piece of information concealed.

'What about Private Larkins?' Matty asked.

'What?' Both women glared at him, obviously annoyed by the interruption.

'The soldier who got pulled out of the window,' he explained. 'The plants attacked him. So they might still attack other people.'

'Well...' Hardy hesitated. 'Actually, he's

unharmed. He was lowered to the ground and then released. It was he who suggested using axes.'

'See?' said Ashna. 'The assassin won't hurt anyone from this time. He'll either use plants again to get past them or he'll try to lure Matthew to him. So all we have to do is keep Matthew safe. We need to keep him here where he can be protected.'

The lieutenant colonel's face tightened. 'Pot plants. Could they—'

'Yes,' answered Ashna, before Hardy could even finish the question. 'Pot plants. Flowers in vases. Any plants. You need to get rid of them.'

'Stay here,' ordered Hardy, as she marched for the door.

'You didn't tell her about the pollen,' said Lucy, once they were alone. 'Why?'

Ashna didn't answer.

'It formed a message,' said Matty, brow furrowed in thought. 'For me.'

'A message?' Lucy didn't understand. She had been watching the pollen released by the flower and although it had formed patterns in the air, there had been no discernible words or letters, as far as she had seen.

Matty nodded slowly. 'It formed symbols. I didn't understand at first. But then they started to sort of make sense.'

'You could read them?' asked Lucy. Was this the

prince's memory coming through? Did this mean Matty was being replaced? The possibility of this upset Lucy. She has grown to like Matty, to consider him a friend, and the idea of him being swapped with someone else was… distressing.

'I couldn't read them as such. They weren't words. But there was a sort of meaning behind them. It's hard to explain. And the meaning sort of started to show through as I looked at them.' He turned to Ashna. 'Why?'

'The royal cypher,' said Ashna, seemingly with reluctance. 'Members of the royal family are taught it at a very young age. A memory so deep that it was not overwritten by your new memories.'

'Could you read it too?' asked Lucy.

'No.'

'But you knew what it was. And you weren't going to tell anyone about it, were you?' accused Lucy.

Ashna didn't respond. Lucy scowled at her. What else was this woman concealing? She thought through everything that had happened. Ashna hadn't said anything about the pollen forming a message. And earlier, she had crushed the first flower that had grown from the chloro-sym.

'You didn't want Matty to get that message,' said Lucy with dawning realisation. 'You were hoping he wouldn't be able to read it.'

Ashna remained stonily silent.

'You're asking a lot of people to trust you and what you've been telling us about this assassin,' said Lucy. 'But you're not telling us everything.' She took a step towards Ashna. 'Time to stop keeping things from us. Time to trust us. Time to trust your Crown Prince.'

Lucy waited, expecting Ashna to finally say something. But no, she maintained her silence.

Turning back to Matty, Lucy asked, 'So, what did the message say?'

'I'm not sure. I'm still trying to piece it all together. There were three symbols. The first one was danger or maybe threat.' He paused. 'Threat of danger.' He nodded to himself. 'Yeah. The second one was home. Coming home. Or going home. Something like that. And the last one was about parents or parent. Helping them. Saving them.'

'So what does it actually mean?' asked Lucy.

'Oh, isn't it obvious?' Ashna finally broke her silence. 'It's a threat. He wants you to go home to save your guardians. As in, he is threatening to hurt or kill them if you don't come home. But you can't go home. Because then he'll kill you.' She huffed. 'It's best to just ignore it. And that…' She looked pointedly at Lucy. '…is why I wasn't going to mention the message.'

Matty's face went white. 'My parents…' His

voice was barely a whisper.

'But you said he wouldn't harm anyone from this time,' said Lucy.

'That's right,' said Ashna, a little too eagerly. 'It's just an idle threat, an attempt to lure the prince out, so we should ignore it and remain here.'

Lucy watched Matty as he looked into Ashna's eyes. 'Why don't I believe you?'

Ashna turned away.

'The assassin knows that you're here,' said Matty, spelling things out logically. 'He knows that, as a fellow time traveller, you would know that he would not do anything to jeopardise the timeline. So he would know that a threat like this, what you just called an idle threat, would not work. So why do it?'

Lucy looked from Ashna to Matty. Her face betrayed guilt. His face was grave. Matty was right, Lucy realised. The assassin would not make an idle threat.

'My parents aren't safe, are they?' said Matty.

'They are not your parents,' replied Ashna, avoiding the question. 'Your parents haven't been born yet. They are in the future.'

'The prince's parents are in the future,' countered Matty. 'But Matthew's parents are here. And I'm still Matthew… at least for now. So just answer my question. Are my parents in danger?'

Ashna sighed. 'Yes, they are in danger.'

'I don't get it,' interrupted Lucy. 'Why are they in danger?'

'It's simple really,' said Ashna. 'The two people he regards as his parents are not meant to be alive. They were meant to have died in a car accident. I saved them, modified their memories, and made them into Matthew's parents. Their continued lives are a risk to the timeline, but an acceptable risk. Their deaths now would not adversely affect the timeline.'

'You're playing with human lives.' Lucy was horrified. 'You're using these people. You saved them from one death to put them at risk of another.'

'I've given them years more than they originally had. I gave them a son, a family. Their accident should have happened because they were distracted while arguing. Arguing about their upcoming divorce. Instead, they've had happy lives.'

In a way, what she was saying sort of made sense to Lucy. And yet it also seemed so wrong. 'You're just trying to come up with justifications.'

'I don't need justification,' responded Ashna. 'I did what I did because it was necessary. And the Franklins benefited from the arrangement.'

Lucy was about to argue. She wanted to argue. She wanted to tell this woman from the future that it wasn't her place to meddle in the lives of people from the past. But she couldn't think of how to say it convincingly.

'It doesn't matter,' said Matty. His face was stony, his eyes unwaveringly locked on to Ashna's. 'I intend to save them.'

MATTY

– CHAPTER SIXTEEN –

PRETEND PARENTS TO WATCH OVER YOU

Matty turned his hands over slowly, studying them. They were actually shaking. He wasn't sure if it was fear or anger or simply that he was overwhelmed. His life had changed so much in such a short amount of time – in the three days since he had met the mysterious Lucy Wilson.

He didn't want to be a prince. He didn't want to return to the future that was supposedly his home. What he wanted was his normal life back – his parents, his friends, his sci-fi books. But apparently, none of that was real.

He clenched his hands into fists, digging the nails into the palms until they hurt. He would not let this future assassin kill his parents, even if it meant sacrificing himself. What did it matter? He wasn't real anyway. Matthew Franklin didn't exist.

He glared at Ashna, who sat on a stool in the

corner of the lab, sulking, back turned to him. She had refused to help him. 'I will not assist you to commit suicide,' she had said, before taking up her current position. He had almost laughed. It was like she had put herself in the naughty corner.

Lucy, meanwhile, paced the room, deep in thought. She had been determined to help, but so far had been unable to come up with any ideas on how to get away from UNIT. There was a guard just outside the door and the whole base was on high alert.

'We could just tell them,' suggested Lucy, suddenly. 'Ask them to help save your parents. I mean, that's what UNIT is supposed to do. Protect Earth. Protect the people. It's usually from aliens trying to invade, but I'm sure an assassin from the future counts too.'

'But what if they don't help?' said Matty. 'Or what if they go rushing in, only to have that assassin kill my parents in retribution.'

'Oh, for goodness' sake,' snapped Ashna, jumping to her feet to face Matty and Lucy. 'Don't you understand? They are dead already!'

'What do you mean?' asked Lucy.

'They should have died in the car accident,' explained Ashna. 'Saving them from that merely delayed the inevitable. They shouldn't be here. So long as the anomaly isn't too great, Time has a way of correcting itself. While I've been watching over the prince, I've also been watching over his substitute parents. Making sure they don't die while we still needed them.' She turned to Matty. 'Have you ever wondered why they don't have a car?'

Matty shrugged. 'They like public transport.'

'It's because if they ever get into a car together, there is a high probability that the car will crash. That they will die. Time doesn't want them here. I am what's keeping them alive. I've made sure they don't own a car. I make sure they don't get into a car together. I watch over them. I nudge and manipulate things to keep them alive. So they can be your pretend parents and watch over you.'

'But... but...' Matty was at a loss for words.

'What do you think will happen when we leave?' asked Ashna.

'Huh?'

'When we leave this time,' said Ashna. 'When I'm no longer here to look after them. What do you think will happen to them?'

Matty's hands began to shake again and he tried to hold back the tears that he felt welling up in his eyes.

'Either now or later,' continued Ashna. 'Either by the assassin's hand or by Time fixing itself. They *will* die. It's just a matter of when.'

Matty wiped at his eyes. 'Then I'm not going

away,' he shouted. 'I'm staying here. I'm going to save them. I'll watch over them. I'll keep them alive.' The floodgates opened, and Matty broke into tears, sobbing uncontrollably.

As he buried his face in his hands, he felt an arm around his shoulders. After a few moments he looked up into Lucy's face.

'I *will* help you,' she said.

LUCY

– CHAPTER SEVENTEEN –

PREPARATIONS

Lucy decided that she had to take matters into her own hands. Ashna wasn't going to be any help. And as for Matty, it was all well and good that he wanted to escape from UNIT and go save his parents, but the truth was that they had no way to do that. There was no way they were going to be able to sneak out of a secret military base. Besides, Lucy wasn't convinced that they should. This was UNIT after all, albeit the Australian branch. This was the organisation that her grandad had helped set up. Lucy believed and trusted in her grandad more than anyone or anything else – that he always did his best to protect people and the earth. Therefore, by extension, she also had to believe and trust in the organisation that he had spent so much of his life devoted to.

Having made her decision, Lucy approached Matty and Ashna. They were arguing, yet again.

'You have no choice,' said Ashna, with exasperation. 'You have to come back home. You do not belong here.'

'I don't care what you say,' countered Matty. 'I *do* belong here. With my parents. And I'm staying. You can't make me come with you.'

'How many times do I have to keep telling you this? They are not your parents. Matthew Franklin does not exist. You are Jaria Dawn Thrise, Crown Prince of the Aslante Separation.'

'I don't care!'

Lucy thought that they were almost at the point of coming to blows.

'As soon as the retrieval pod arrives, we are leaving,' said Ashna, with an assured finality. 'So long as you are with me when I activate it, you won't have a choice.'

'You can't do that!'

Ashna turned her back on him, signalling the end of the dispute. Matty was left red-faced with frustration.

Lucy took him by the arm and led him to the opposite end of the room. 'Do you trust me?' she asked quietly.

'Um, I guess so.'

The sound of Lieutenant Colonel Hardy's approaching voice could be heard in the corridor outside.

'No. Not *I guess so*. I need to know for sure, one way or the other.' She glanced at the door, then looked at him pointedly. 'Do you trust me?'

He gazed into her eyes and she felt so many unspoken things pass between them. Then he gave her a little smile. 'Yes!'

The door opened.

'Good.' Lucy patted his arm. ''Cause this is our only option.'

Hardy entered the room with a dark-skinned woman in a white lab coat who she introduced as their science advisor Doctor Tahnee Mullina.

Lucy grinned. Finally, someone who wasn't white. The science advisor's long, dark brown, wavy hair was pulled back in an unruly ponytail that reached halfway down her back, the bright orange scrunchie barely holding it all together. Her smile was as sunny at the yellow top that was visible beneath the lab coat.

'G'day everyone,' she said. 'Boss Lady has filled me in on what's happening and I've got to say that I am over-the-moon excited about all this. Actual time travellers. So! Freaking! Cool! Not to mention plants that move around on their own and attack people. Our Pommy counterparts have apparently encountered both before, but this is a first for us here down under. I have so many questions for you I hardly know where to start.' She was talking at a million miles an hour, her excitement bubbling over. 'I also have some thoughts on how we can deal with this assassin. We have equipment that can register and track disturbances in time. Now, if we were to modify it, we could—'

'You do not need to deal with the assassin!' Ashna advanced on the newcomer. 'We just need to stay away from the assassin until we can return to our own time. Do you understand? And no questions! Knowledge of the future is dangerous.'

Dr Mullina seemed taken aback and Lieutenant Colonel Hardy looked ready to argue. But Lucy stepped forward.

'Just ignore her,' she said quickly to Hardy and Mullina, before they could start another argument. 'She doesn't speak for me or Matty. We don't need her. I've got something to tell you.'

'What?' thundered Ashna.

'Huh?' said Matty, confusion on his face.

'Trust me!' Lucy said gently, making eye contact with Matty. Then glancing at Ashna she added, 'And you can just shut up. We're handling this from now on.'

Ashna looked ready to explode, her face turning the colour of beetroot, eyes bugging out in fury. But before she could say anything, the lieutenant colonel intervened. 'One word from you and I'll have you removed from the room under armed guard.'

Lucy smirked before continuing. 'I'm from 2020 and I *am* Brigadier Lethbridge-Stewart's granddaughter. I trust my grandfather. I know that he was involved with creating UNIT, so I'm going to trust you. Okay?'

Hardy and Mullina nodded.

'Matty and Ashna are from further in the future than me – much further. As far as I can gather, their people are genetically modified and somehow mixed with plants. But this assassin is like… super modified. That's why he can control plants. I don't think these two can do that.' She quickly turned to Matty. 'You can't, can you?'

Matty shrugged, then shook his head, and Lucy turned back to Hardy and Mullina.

'Right. So, this assassin is out to get Matty. But the assassin can't get in here without risking the lives of people. So he's trying to lure Matty out of here. In that last attack with the bushes, he sent a message.'

By three o'clock that afternoon (two fifty-eight, to be exact, which Matty and his digital watch insisted on being), Lucy found herself in the back of the military van again, with Matty and a disgruntled Ashna, who had insisted on coming along so she could be near her prince if/when the retrieval pod arrived. Lucy briefly wondered what the pod would be like and how it would arrive. She imagined a giant plant seedpod appearing out of nowhere, splitting open to swallow them up, then disappearing again.

This time the three of them were accompanied in the back of the van by Dr Mullina, rather than by soldiers. The UNIT troops were in a second van following close behind theirs.

In her hand, Lucy clutched an envelope. And then she remembered…

She remembered getting the Polaroid of a boy in the post. She remembered falling into the darkness.

Matty had provided her with the Space/Time Books address and she had written a short note telling Marvin that he had to post her that photo so that it would reach her in Ogmore-By-Sea on 27th February 2020.

The van pulled over and the driver twisted around to look into the back. 'Letterbox is just outside, Miss.'

'Thanks.'

Lucy hopped out and stood by the large red box, holding onto the letter. It was funny how time travel worked. Here she was, about to post a letter to prompt someone else to post her a photo in the future year of 2020, so that she would time travel back to 1985, where the photo would be taken… starting the whole cycle off again.

But she knew it would work. She had witnessed similar weird time loops with her grandfather when they had travelled back in time to his childhood. Still, it made her head hurt to think too much about it.

MATTY

– CHAPTER EIGHTEEN –

SOLDIERS IN SUBURBIA

Thursday 22 August 1985. 4:11pm. Matty used the edge of his t-shirt to clean the screen of his digital watch as the van brought them ever closer to their destination. He loved the fact that it told him the date as well as the time. It had a stopwatch function and multiple alarms. Oh, and it was shock-resistant and waterproof too. He thought about how his parents must have paid a lot for it. But it was a special present, because they loved him. A present for his fifteenth birthday.

A bunch of different thoughts collided in his head.

Would his parents still love him if they found out that he was from the future? If they discovered that he wasn't really their son? If they got their real memories back?

Was he actually fifteen? Sure, he wasn't born in 1970, because he was from the future. But was the twelfth of February still his birthday? Or was it a different day. Maybe he was really sixteen? Or seventeen? Or fourteen? He wasn't so happy about the possibility of being younger.

Were there digital watches in the future, he wondered. Surely there must be. Just more sophisticated. After all, people would still need to know the time and date. Maybe in the future, a digital watch would be more than a watch. Maybe it would also be a videophone? Wouldn't that be cool? Maybe in the future, everyone would have digital watches.

The van pulled up at the top of Matty's street, breaking him out of his thoughts.

'Rightio,' said Dr Mullina. 'We've parked two blocks from the house.' She handed little grey boxes with clasps on them to Matty and Lucy. 'Clip these on to your belts. They'll allow us to track you and to gather readings. There's also inbuilt microphones so we can listen in. So if you need help and want the cavalry to come marching in, just sing out.' She glanced at Ashna. 'Sorry. The budget only stretched to two.'

Ashna glared in silence.

'But you get the flamethrowers,' continued Dr Mullina enthusiastically.

'Joy.' Ashna's response was completely deadpan.

The back of the van swung open to reveal Lieutenant Colonel Hardy standing outside.

'I don't like this,' she stated flatly. 'I would much prefer to let the troops handle it.'

'Have you been able to reach my parents?' asked Matty, anxiously.

'No,' admitted Hardy. 'They both seem to have left their places of employment early today.'

'Which means they must be at home,' said Matty, 'with the assassin. So if UNIT attacked, he might harm my parents.'

'Which is why we're letting you go in on your own,' grumbled Hardy. 'But I still don't like it.'

'Well, I don't like any of this,' said Ashna. 'This is a mistake.'

'We still have time to mount an assault,' suggested Hardy. Matty thought her eyes looked curiously pleading. Not something he would have expected from a hardened military officer. 'My troops are ready.'

'No!' Matty was emphatic. His parents' safety was what mattered most to him. He wouldn't risk their lives.

Everyone eyed each other for a good half minute without further comment, before Dr Mullina finally spoke. 'Well, we should probably get this show on the road then, eh?'

They all climbed out of the van and one of the UNIT men fitted out Ashna with the flamethrower, a metal backpack arrangement with a hose and gun-like attachment. It reminded Matty of the toy water pistols with backpack water storage he'd seen advertised on television during the Saturday morning cartoons – but less colourful and more deadly.

Three soldiers from the second vehicle assembled beside them and saluted Lieutenant Colonel Hardy. One of them had a flamethrower on his back, the other two had big guns – automatic rifles of some variety, he assumed. Matty wondered what the residents thought of all this activity in their street. It must be an unusual sight, two military vans with soldiers and some kids. He thought it a bit strange that no one was coming out of their homes to investigate.

'You men are with me,' said Hardy, returning the salute, then turning to Dr Mullina. 'Doctor, you'll monitor things from here. I'm leaving two soldiers with you.'

'Wait,' said Matty. 'We're going into the house alone. It's bad enough Ashna is coming along. Soldiers are not a good idea.' In his mind's eye he saw the assassin panicking at the sight of the military and killing his parents in retribution for bringing them along.

'Relax,' responded Hardy soothingly, glancing up at the sky. 'We'll accompany you to the property, then wait outside.'

'Oh. Okay.' Matty figured that was an acceptable compromise. He followed Hardy's gaze up to the winter sky. Although there was a scattering of light grey cloud against the blue, there was no rain. A chilly breeze made him shiver.

Returning his gaze to the street, he noticed that it was unusually empty for a Thursday afternoon. Kids should have been returning from school. He glanced at the house that they had parked beside. The front door was open.

'Where is everyone?' he asked slowly.

'Evacuated,' answered Hardy. 'On the pretext of a gas leak.'

'But what if the assassin noticed?' Matty's voice had gone up a notch, visions of his parents being killed filling his mind again.

'No alternative,' said Hardy. 'We could not put the local residents in danger. It is our job to protect them.'

'But…' began Matty.

'It's a moot point,' said Hardy, bringing the exchange to an end. 'What's done is done.'

Matty's jaw tensed. Had all this been a mistake?

'Shouldn't we get going?' suggested Lucy.

'Yes, I suppose we should,' said Hardy, again glancing up at the sky.

Matty, Lucy and Ashna set off down the street, Hardy and her troops marching a few paces behind them. He eyed the silent houses as they passed, wondering where the people had been evacuated to. They had barely gone a few metres when he heard a distant sound. He didn't pay much attention to it at first, but as it increased in volume, he began to search around for its source. Glancing up, he saw a helicopter approaching. Khaki green in colour, it was zooming through the sky from the direction of the city and descending towards them.

'What the…'

Matty fought the urge to duck as it passed over them and headed for his house.

'Oh no.'

He turned back to stare at Lieutenant Colonel Hardy. She looked Matty straight in the eye. 'I'm sorry.'

LUCY

– CHAPTER NINETEEN –

REPEATEDLY

Lucy rounded on Hardy. 'What have you done?' She could barely get the words out, she was shaking so hard. What she really wanted to do was hit this woman. Physical violence was not usually something that Lucy would consider, but she was furious. She had trusted Hardy. She had trusted UNIT. She had trusted her grandad's legacy. This betrayal stung more than she could put into words.

'I really am sorry.' Hardy didn't flinch. 'I really couldn't send children into a potential hostage situation without first having exhausted all other options.'

'A helicopter is your first option?'

'No,' admitted Hardy. 'This is our next-to-last option. While we were getting you ready, we were actually providing time for our first option.'

Lucy couldn't believe it. She clenched her fists and her jaw, trying to get herself under control.

'We tried sending in a small strike team while we were en route.'

'And?' Lucy's voice was quavery.

'And we lost contact with them almost immediately after they entered the property. The only useful information we were able to get is that the garden is like a jungle and that it's... moving.'

'So, if the 'copter is next-to-last... what's your last option?' asked Lucy.

Hardy gave her a steely gaze. 'We are.'

Lucy turned around to see the helicopter was now circling Matty's house. Her heart sank. 'I trusted you,' she whispered.

'Alistair may have made a different decision were he here,' said Hardy. 'But this is my command, not his.'

Did Lucy detect a hint of regret in the lieutenant colonel's voice?

'You should never have revealed anything to them,' snarled Ashna, glaring at Lucy. 'This could cause untold damage to the timeline.'

Lucy looked at Matty and caught his eye, inclining her head towards the house. Matty nodded. And the two of them took off, racing down the street.

'No!' shouted Hardy.

Lucy checked behind her to see Hardy and her men in pursuit, along with Ashna. She was determined to get there ahead of them. She and Matty might be able to salvage the situation if they could get into the house before the helicopter did whatever it was that it was going to do.

'Look!' called Matty, stopping.

Lucy stopped also, as did their pursuers. Everyone's eyes went to the helicopter. The door was open and there were figures in the doorway. The helicopter was descending.

'What's happening?' demanded Lucy. 'Are they trying to land?'

'That helo is carrying a tank of a new experimental weed killer,' explained Hardy. 'They are going to spray the property.'

As they watched, Lucy could see the men in the doorway lowering a hose. But before the poison could be sprayed, a vine shot up from below. It wrapped around the hose, reached into the helicopter and pulled out a large metal drum, presumably containing the weed killer. On its way out, the drum knocked into one of the men, causing him to fall from the doorway. Luckily, he managed to grasp hold of the landing struts.

Lucy gasped.

The vine disappeared behind the tall green fence with the metal drum, as the soldier dangled from the struts by one arm. Despite the chilly weather, Lucy's palms were sweaty as she watched the helicopter. The soldier still in the doorway lowered a rope to the one on the strut. He clipped it to his harness and let go, now dangling in the air. Slowly he was pulled back up.

'Well, that's that,' said Lucy.

'Hardly,' said the lieutenant colonel. 'It's not over yet.'

Lucy squinted to see what was happening. The two soldiers had disappeared inside the helicopter, but after a minute, they were back in the doorway… jumping out. Suspended in the air on ropes, they began to descend towards Matty's front garden.

'Idiots!' grumbled Ashna.

Lucy could see equipment on their backs and something gun-like in their hands. Fire rushed from them down to the garden.

'Flamethrowers,' gasped Lucy. 'They've got flamethrowers.'

'But my parents are in there,' yelled Matty, panic-stricken, as he took off at a run.

Lucy bolted after him, and the others after her.

And then she felt it. That repeating sensation. Her right trainer hit the footpath repeatedly on the one step.

She heard Hardly exclaim, 'What the heck?' from behind her.

'Something's happening,' said Matty.

'Time distortion,' called Ashna.

Lucy stopped and looked up. Something was wrong.

Then she took that same step again.

'What the heck?'

'Something's happening.'

'Time distortion.'

Lucy stopped and looked up.

The two soldiers jumped from the helicopter and descended towards the garden. Fire roared from their flamethrowers… but never reached the target, because…

The two soldiers jumped from the helicopter and descended towards the garden. Fire roared from their flamethrowers… but never reached the target, because…

The two soldiers jumped from the helicopter and descended towards the garden. Fire roared from their flamethrowers… but never reached the target, because…

Lucy gasped and looked at Ashna.

'Time loop,' she said matter-of-factly. 'It stops them without hurting them… or the timeline.'

'This is our chance,' said Matty. Then he took off again.

Lucy followed without hesitation.

'Wait!' she heard Hardy shout from behind. 'You can't just—'

Lucy kept running. She was not going to let

Hardy stop her.

'Wait! You can't just—'

No matter how many times she was shouted at, Lucy wasn't about to stop.

'Wait! You can't just—'

Huh? Lucy glanced back over her shoulder as she ran.

'Wait! You can't just—'

The lieutenant colonel and her soldiers glitched, like a faulty computer game.

'Wait! You can't just—'

They did it again. Ashna had stopped beside them, watching apparently unaffected.

'Wait! You can't just—'

Lucy smacked into Matty, who had stopped ahead of her to turn back.

'Wait! You can't just—'

Ashna laughed at the soldiers and strode over to Lucy and Matty. 'Now *they're* caught in a time loop.' Then she added, almost to herself, 'This must be taking an enormous amount of effort.'

'Why aren't we?' said Matty, asking the question that Lucy was thinking.

'There are a few possibilities,' said Ashna. 'The assassin has limited energy to maintain time loops, so has only directed them at immediate threats. Or we're immune because we don't belong in this time. Or…'

Lucy looked up to see a bird flapping its way through the same flight path repeatedly. She could feel a sense of dread spread through her, chilling her more than the cold breeze. 'Or it's a trap just for us and he's keeping everything else out.'

MATTY

– CHAPTER TWENTY –

INTO THE JUNGLE

Matty took a deep breath and yanked open the gate. He gasped. When Hardy had said that the garden was a jungle, he hadn't really thought about what she'd meant. He'd always considered it a bit of a jungle because it was so overgrown. But now, staring into the vegetation, he realised that she had meant it literally. It was now so thick and tangled that he couldn't see the house.

'Wow!' said Lucy.

'He's obviously made himself at home,' added Ashna.

The plants parted a little as Matty took a step forward.

Ashna readied the flamethrower. 'Perhaps I should go first and clear a path.'

'No.' Matty did not want to take any chances. 'I'll go.' He took another step and the plants withdrew a little more. It was as if they were inviting him in.

He could feel Lucy sticking close behind him, and assumed Ashna was behind her. He began to walk slowly, the vegetation moving and parting around him.

'They're closing us in,' said Ashna from behind.

Matty looked back to see that the plants had blocked off access to the gate.

Ashna held up the flamethrower's nozzle and placed her finger on the trigger. But that's as far as she got. With lightning speed, vines and branches and leaves were surrounding her, winding themselves about the nozzle and yanking it away. And she was being lifted up, encased in a cocoon of green until just her face was visible, hanging in the trees. She struggled, gasped and grunted, trying to free herself.

More vines snaked towards Matty and Lucy, snatching Doctor Mullina's tracking devices from their belts.

Then a flower bloomed in front of Ashna. As its petals opened, a puff of pollen wafted into her face. She closed her eyes and went limp.

'OMG! Is she dead?' gasped Lucy.

But then Ashna began to snore.

'Not dead, then.' Lucy looked at Matty. 'Do we go on?'

He nodded and they continued, the plants creating a passage in front of them, then growing over it again as they passed.

Something caught his attention up ahead. There were faces… faces hanging in the foliage above, like bizarre Christmas decorations. 'Oh no!' he gasped, pointing up.

'Must be Hardy's strike team,' said Lucy.

Three faces, cocooned in green, a wilted flower in front of each, slept peacefully amongst the plants.

Matty continued to lead the way, until the plants revealed the front porch. He climbed the three rickety wooden steps up to the door, which hung open. Inside was more green. Grass grew from the carpet, vines hung from the ceiling and moss covered the walls. Trees and shrubs lined the corridor, the tallest of which had broken through the ceiling. It wasn't as dense as outside.

'Hello!' Matty called.

'Matthew?' cried a distant voice.

'Mum?' said Matty.

'Down the corridor,' said Lucy.

They made their way through the interior jungle, past the doors to Matty's bedroom and the spare room where Lucy had been sleeping. Matty had a hard time reconciling his memories of home with this house he now moved through. The very feel of the place was different. Moisture dripped from the greenery, humidity hung in the air, and it all seemed like it was about to close in on him. Despite his love of plants, he found it oppressive… menacing.

At the end of the corridor was his mum and dad's room. He went to push the door open, but it moved before he could touch it.

'Hello! Is there someone out there?' There was an air of desperation to his dad's voice.

'It's me,' he said, racing into the room.

'Matthew!' cried his mum.

Just like Ashna and the strike team outside, his mum and dad were cocooned in pods, hanging from the ceiling on vines, wilted flowers in front of their faces. Matty realised they must have been asleep, but had perhaps been woken by his call when they entered the house.

'You're okay.' Matty's voice cracked with relief.

'I don't understand what's going on.' His dad's voice was panicky. 'We came home to find plants everywhere.'

'And they were moving,' added his mum.

'And then they attacked us,' continued his dad. 'What's going on, son?'

Two new flowers bloomed, one in front of each of them, and blew sleeping pollen into their faces, silencing them.

'The bed,' said Lucy from behind him.

His parents' bed was covered in a mishmash of plants – moss and vines and creepers and grass and leaves and succulents all melded together into some sort of hybrid – with another cocoon in the centre.

As Matty watched, it split open, falling away. Standing in the middle was the assassin from the future. He wasn't wearing green clothes like Matty had thought when they first met in the city; rather it was a covering of vegetable matter, hundreds of tiny leaves growing from his body like hairs. He looked older than he had the last time. Middle-aged. But his eyes still glowed with an eerie green colour.

'Let my parents go,' demanded Matty.

Vines slithered above him, and his parents' cocoons were lowered from the ceiling. As they fell open, his mum and dad slumped to the floor.

'Are they okay?' He ran to them, crouching down to check their breathing

'They are unharmed,' said the assassin, his voice measured and even. 'They will wake once this is all over.'

Matty stared back at this strange person, wondering what he should do. Lucy edged herself over to stand beside him. As he stood, he felt her tentatively take his hand. 'What do we do now?' he whispered from the corner of his mouth. Lucy gave his hand a gently squeeze, then let go to boldly take a step towards the assassin.

'My name is Lucy Wilson,' she said. 'And I will not let you kill my friend.'

The man gave her a puzzled look. 'I am not here

to kill anyone.'

'Hang about? What?' Now it was Lucy's turn to be puzzled.

'Aren't you here to assassinate me?' asked Matty.

'No, my prince. I'm here to return you to your throne. Did you not get my message?'

'Um...' Matty gaped. None of this made any sense to him. 'But...' He didn't know what to say. Or what to think. 'Ah...'

'Your message?' Lucy's voice was indignant. 'The one in which you threatened to kill Matty's parents if he didn't come home?'

'The message,' corrected the man, voice still even, 'indicated that he was in danger here in this time and that he needed to return home to his own time in order to save his parents. It appears you have misinterpreted it.' He paused as if considering something. 'Perhaps I should have been clearer?'

'So, who exactly are you?' demanded Lucy.

'I am Royal Guardian Morai,' he answered.

'But... we... we were told that you were here to assassinate me.' Matty finally found his voice. 'Ashna. She said that she was my guardian and that she was protecting me from you.'

'You have been misinformed,' said Morai. 'She is not your guardian. She is your kidnapper.'

LUCY

– CHAPTER TWENTY-ONE –

MISINFORMED

After what had happened with UNIT, Lucy wasn't keen on trusting anyone else – least of all a plant person from the future, who held several hostages, constrained even more people in a time loop and controlled all the surrounding vegetation to boot.

'How can you expect us to believe you?' she demanded. 'You know, given everything you've done.'

'It's the truth,' he replied simply.

'But you've attacked us,' said Matty. 'You kidnapped my parents.'

'And you've trapped all those people in a time loop,' added Lucy.

'I have not attacked you,' said Morai. 'I have not attacked anyone, except Ashna. I am sorry about your parents, but keeping them here was for their own protection. As for the time loop… it's a nonaggressive form of protection from those seeking to harm me. No one will be damaged by it, and they will all be released once my mission is complete.'

'Your mission?' whispered Matty.

'Yes. As I already said, I am here to return you to the throne, my prince.'

'All right, all right,' said Lucy, trying to get control of the situation. 'We need some more information here. Ashna told us that Matty... uh, the prince was brought here, to this time, to hide him from assassins.'

'That information is misleading,' said Morai. 'Jaria Dawn Thrice is a direct decedent of the royal line, and hence Crown Prince. The queen is due to retire on her seventieth birthday, and he is to be crowned head of state. But he was kidnapped and hidden in the past to persuade the queen to name a new successor. If he does not return, the crown will pass to an offshoot of the royal line, headed by Lainor Dusk Septence. His ascension would be divisive at best. We are already on the brink of civil war. The return of the prince is imperative to the survival of the Aslante Separation.'

'What do you think?' asked Matty, coming to stand beside Lucy.

'I...' Lucy didn't know. Matty had trusted her decision to involve UNIT, and that hadn't exactly worked out like she had hoped. What right did she have to give him advice about this? 'I think this is your call.'

Eyes distant even though he was facing her, he slowly nodded.

'What about my parents?' he said, facing Morai.

'The people you refer to as you parents are not really—'

'Yes, I know,' Matty interrupted, a harshness edging his voice. 'I know they're just random people who were supposed to die, who've had their memories altered, who think that I'm their son. But…' His voice softened. 'I care about them. I love them. And I want to make sure, no matter what else happens, that they'll be okay.'

'Interesting,' said Morai. He waited a moment before answering. 'I will not harm them. Once we are gone, they will awaken.'

'But what happens to them if I go?' asked Matty. 'Do they get their old memories back or do they keep their new ones? Do they continue to live, or do they die in a car crash like they were originally supposed to?'

Morai tilted his head as if considering something he had not previously given any thought to. 'I do not know.' He paused, titling his head to the other side. 'I have little information on this time period. I have no information on these people and their lives. I do not know if they will live or die.'

'I will not leave unless I know they will be safe.' There was a fierce determination on Matty's face that Lucy had not seen before. She couldn't imagine what he must be going through at that moment. How would she feel if she was suddenly told that her parents weren't really her parents? What would she do?

'If these people are, as you say, meant to have died in this timeline,' said Morai, 'then there is no need for them to continue in this timeline.'

'I will not stand by and let them die,' shouted Matty.

'Theoretically,' said Morai, 'they could accompany us to the future. Their absence from this timeline would return it to its correct alignment.'

Matty's eyes lit up. 'Do you promise to take them with us?'

'If that is what it takes for you to return, then you have my word that they shall accompany us.'

'Okay then,' said Matty. 'I'll come with you.'

Lucy placed a hand on his shoulder. 'Are you sure?'

'No,' said Matty, quietly. 'I'm not sure. But what other option do I have? With everything that's happened, I can't really stay here, can I? This way, at least they'll be safe.'

'Um…' said Lucy. 'That's assuming this guy is telling the truth.'

'I believe him. I mean, if he really was an assassin like Ashna said he was, then wouldn't he have killed me by now?'

Lucy scrutinised their surroundings – they were standing in a room filled with plants; plants that were at Morai's beck and call; plants that could, at any moment, twist themselves around Matty and squeeze the life out of him. She had to admit, what he said made sense. 'Okay.'

Matty turned to face Morai. 'So, how do we do this?'

'The retrieval pod has been implanted in me.'

'That sounds uncomfortable,' quipped Lucy, hoping to lighten the mood.

'It was almost unbearable,' said Morai.

Lucy saw the pain in his eyes. 'Sorry, I didn't mean to…'

Her voice trailed away as she saw his chest bulge. His leaf-like covering was undulating as a fist-sized lump protruded from him. The leaves parted and what appeared to be a seedpod sprouted from his chest. Lucy wondered how something so small was going to transport four people.

Morai gasped as it detached itself and fell into his outstretched hand. He held it up to show Matty. 'If you are ready, we can leave now.'

'Oh, right now?' Matty seemed suddenly uncertain. But then he looked down at his parents, unconscious on the floor, and nodded. 'Yeah, I'm ready.'

Morai dropped the pod and screamed, the vegetation around him suddenly thrashing about.

Lucy felt panic rise up inside her. Was this supposed to be happening?

MATTY

– CHAPTER TWENTY-TWO –

THIS ENDS NOW

Matty watched Morai drop to his knees, a piercing shriek issuing from the Royal Guardian's gaping mouth.

'What's happening?' shouted Matty.

'I don't know,' Lucy yelled back.

Around them, the plants were all moving, slowly edging their way towards the wailing Royal Guardian. Morai snapped his mouth shut and clenched his teeth. His eyes closed and his whole body tensed. It looked to Matty as if he were trying to endure some sort of horrible pain.

'Being… attacked…' He managed to spit the words out between gasps.

'Attacked?' gulped Matty. 'By who?'

'Maybe the UNIT people have broken through the time loop?' suggested Lucy.

Matty noticed that Morai's breathing was becoming more regulated, shifting from ragged gasps to short, sharp breaths – in through the nose, out through the mouth. 'Time loop… holding…' he said between breaths. 'Ashna… trying to… attack with… local vegetation…'

'She must have escaped,' said Lucy. 'But how's she doing this?'

'Can't hold… two fronts…'

'What does that mean?' asked Matty, looking to Lucy.

'I think it means he can't hold the time loop in place and fight off Ashna.'

'Yes…' gasped Morai, his breathing becoming ragged again.

Matty's eyes flitted about the room in panic. The plants were still making their way towards Morai, the closest wrapping around him, squeezing, pulling, smothering…

'We've got to stop her!' Matty turned and ran out into the corridor.

It was a similar scene out there, the plants all trembling as if trying to resist some unseen force, while edging their way towards the door. Before he could go any further, a burst of flame exploded at the far end of the corridor, vines withering and dying, leaves turning to ash, grass disappearing in a blaze. Morai's accompanying cry echoed from the room behind him.

Matty instinctively held up an arm to shield his

face from the blast of hot air.

As the flames dissipated and he lowered his arm, Ashna stepped into view. She held the flamethrower at the ready, the pilot flame visible at the nozzle. She was covered in branches, wrapped and twisted around her like some kind of bizarre armour. And her eyes blazed with a vibrant green.

'I'm back!' she snarled.

'You lied to me!' Matty felt foolish. He had swallowed everything Ashna had fed him.

'Not about everything,' she retorted. 'You are a prince. I have been hiding and protecting you. Your parents in this time were meant to die in a car crash. And I am taking you back to your own time. The only thing I lied about was my motivation. I'm not a Royal Guardian, I'm a freelancer in the employ of Lainor Dusk Septence.'

'Best way to hide a lie,' said Lucy from behind him, 'is to wrap it up in the truth.'

'I'm going to stop you,' declared Matty.

'What? Really?' Ashna did a mock double take. 'I thought I was the one with the flamethrower.' She pulled the trigger and torched the bush to the right of her. Morai screamed again.

Matty was determined to stop her, but he didn't know how.

'How did you escape?' asked Lucy.

'Blood!'

'What?'

'My blood,' said Ashna, with a laugh. 'I don't have the same control over plants that this royalist does. But I have some. And without my chloro-sym, the only way I could amplify it was with my blood. My genetic modifications make me immune to the sleeping pollen. After you were gone from view, I struggled just enough to cut my arm on a branch. I was able to use that to control that one plant. Morai was so preoccupied with you that I was able to slowly spread my control to the surrounding plants. Morai may be stronger than I, but he's also trying to maintain a massive time loop around this property, so he's weakened. And I can weaken him even more.' She shot another burst of fire, this time at the ceiling. Morai's shrieks could be heard as vines were engulfed in flame.

'Enough talk. This ends now. The retrieval pod has arrived and you, your highness, are coming with me.'

A vine snaked out from behind Ashna carrying a seedpod identical to Morai's.

'No!' Matty felt the defiance coursing through him. He had no intention of giving in. 'I am not leaving my parents.'

Ashna hoisted up the flamethrower and aimed. 'I want you to come with me. But I can't let you fall into Morai's hands. So I will kill you if I have to. As

I said, this ends now. But how it ends is up to you.'

Matty froze. Should he go with Ashna?

Suddenly Lucy threw her arms around him, enveloping him in a hug.

LUCY

– CHAPTER TWENTY-THREE –

UNIT

Lucy held on to Matty, hugging him fiercely. 'I have an idea,' she whispered in his ear. 'Pretend to go along with what she wants. But delay her as much as you can.'

'Very touching,' called Ashna. 'But it changes nothing.'

Lucy released Matty and stepped back. Matty moved forward to stand between Lucy and Ashna. 'How is this going to work?' he asked.

Lucy edged back towards the bedroom door as Ashna spoke. 'What's the point in me explaining? Without your true memories it's not as if you're going to understand. So just come here.'

As Matty took another tentative step towards Ashna, Lucy slipped through the doorway into the bedroom.

Morai was sprawled on the plant-covered bed, wrapped in vegetation, gasping with the strain of fighting off Ashna's attack while also holding off the UNIT troops. Lucy rushed to his side and dropped to her knees.

'You need to release the time loop,' she said.

Morai's eyes snapped open and he shook his sweat-soaked head.

'Ashna is about to use a retrieval pod to take Matty away,' said Lucy, as Morai's expression became more frantic. 'You can't stop her while you're also holding that time loop in place. You need to let the loop go and save Matty.'

'No...' gasped Morai. 'Soldiers... attack...'

'The soldiers are here because they think you're a threat. But you're not. Ashna is the threat. If you release the soldiers you can stop Ashna. I'll take care of UNIT.' Lucy pictured herself trying to get past Ashna to get to the lieutenant colonel. 'I need a clear path out to the street. Can you give me that?'

Morai licked his lips and nodded.

'Oh and also, I'm going to go run right past Ashna, so can you, I don't know, make sure she doesn't barbecue me with the flamethrower?'

Morai's eyes were closed again, his face contorted in concentration. Lucy hoped that he'd be able to follow through. As she got to her feet, she saw that the plants around him were already loosening their grip. *That's a good sign,* she thought.

Leaving Morai to handle his battle, she went off

to face her own. Coming out into the corridor, she saw that Morai was now fighting back, and so was Matty. As the plants around them fought each other, Matty and Ashna were grappling for control of the flamethrower, the retrieval pod lying on the grass. Ashna managed to press the trigger, and flames gushed from the nozzle, incinerating the moss on the wall. But Matty fought to redirect the fire to the retrieval pod. Ashna released the trigger just in time.

Lucy wanted to stop and help Matty, but she knew she couldn't. She had to get to the lieutenant colonel before the UNIT troops attacked. But she could, perhaps, grab the retrieval pod on the way. She sprinted down the corridor, but as she neared the pod, another burst of flame shot to the side of her. She couldn't risk picking it up – the extra second it would take could end up with her getting fried.

As she ran along the corridor, she aimed her foot and kicked out at the pod. The green sphere went sailing through the air and slammed into the wall by the front door.

'Noooooo!' Ashna yelled, as the pod split open and fell to the floor, a mass of vines erupting from within it.

Lucy didn't look back. She dashed out the door into the yard. The plants outside were still, many of them burnt and smouldering. The three soldiers from the strike team were slumped on the grass, released from their cocoons. Looking up she saw the two soldiers descending from the helicopter, flamethrowers extended. She waved her arms at them and shouted, 'Stop! Go back!' but knew there was no chance of them hearing her over the sound of the rotors. She ran for the gate, pulling and tearing at the now limp vines that covered it.

She managed to clear the gate, push it open and run outside, slamming straight into a confused Lieutenant Colonel Hardy, flanked by her three soldiers.

'Call off the helicopter,' yelled Lucy.

'What?' demanded Hardy. 'Explain yourself.'

'Please, trust me,' panted Lucy. 'Call off the helicopter. Then I'll explain.'

For a moment, Lucy thought it was a lost cause, but then she saw something in Hardy's eyes. There was still a chance.

'If you have any respect for my grandfather, please trust me.'

The woman wavered for a moment, then grabbed the radio from her belt.

'Kanga to Flying Fox One. Abort mission. Repeat abort.'

Lucy watched with relief as the helicopter, the two soldiers still dangling from it, veered away from the house.

'Now what in the blazes is going on?'

'Thank you,' said Lucy. 'We had it all wrong. There is no assassin. The plants are no longer a danger.'

'No assassin?' asked Hardy. 'Then what—'

'It's Ashna,' interrupted Lucy. 'She's been lying the entire time. She kidnapped Matty from the future. That guy in green that landed in the city, he's not here to kill Matty, he's here to rescue him and take him home.'

'I knew there was something off about that woman,' declared Hardy. 'So, what are we supposed to do?'

'We've got to help Matty. He's fighting with Ashna. And she's still got the flamethrower.' And with that, Lucy ran back into the garden.

'With me,' she heard Hardy ordering her men from behind.

Lucy raced through the yard and onto the front porch. She stopped dead.

Through the doorway she could see the retrieval pod was going crazy. The vines were waving about grabbing onto things — plants, light fittings, bits of debris — and pulling them towards the centre of the tentacle-like mass, where a swirl of light blazed. Each time something was pulled in, it touched the light and vanished in a flare of brightness. Taken to the future, she assumed.

'Help!' yelled Matty

Beyond the pod, Matty and Ashna were both in the grip of vines, slowly being drawn to the light.

'Stand back!' Hardy stepped forward and aimed her pistol. She fired. Once. Twice. A third time. But the bullets simply disappeared into the light. 'Damn. Let's try something with a little more kick.' She moved out of the way.

'Corporal Jarrah!' she barked, and one of her soldiers came forward raising his automatic rifle. 'Vine thing with the light. Five rounds rapid!'

Jarrah let loose. The bullets ripped through the vines, severing a number of them, including the one that had Matty. The boy immediately sprang to his feet and backed away. Ashna, who was still being pulled towards the pod, made a grab for him but he managed to dodge her.

Before Lucy's astonished eyes more vines grew from the pod to replace those that had gone. One of them shot forward, and seized the weapon from Jarrah's hands, pulling it into the light, where it flared and disappeared.

'I hoped to avoid this, given the enclosed space,' said Hardy. 'But, needs must. Private Wilson. Torch it!'

Wilson stepped forward, flamethrower at the ready. Lucy, Hardy and Jarrah, retreated a few steps as fire engulfed the pod and its vines. A shrill whining filled the air, like thousands of cicadas screeching at day's end. The vines withdrew into the pod, withering as they went, and with them went Ashna.

Wilson switched off the flames, but the pod and vines continued to burn. *It's as if they are covered in petrol,* thought Lucy, the way they roared with flames.

'Help meeeee!' Ashna screamed as she was pulled through the flames and into the light.

The light flared with so much brilliance that Lucy had to close her eyes, and still the brightness seared through her eyelids. When, at last, it faded and she was able to see again, the pod, the vines, and Ashna were gone, a smouldering patch on the floor in their place.

'I have no idea how I'm going to write up this report,' said Hardy, as she unclipped her radio. Lucy almost burst into laughter in response.

'Kanga to Flying Fox One. You still in the area? Over.'

'Flying Fox One to Kanga,' came the crackly response. 'We're still circling. What's going on? There was a light coming from the property. Over.'

'Threat has been neutralised. You can land the helo and come help with the cleanup.'

Turning away from the UNIT personnel, Lucy realised that Matty was no longer in the corridor. He must have gone back to Morai in the bedroom. As she went to check, she noticed with alarm that the vegetation was starting to move again. A flower began to grow from between the remaining blades of grass. As she walked along the corridor, more flowers sprung up. One of them released a little burst of pollen.

Quickly, Lucy covered her nose and mouth with the crook of her elbow and held her breath. She glanced over her shoulder to see Hardy and the soldier dropping to their knees, gasping for breath. Now what?

She ran for the bedroom door.

MATTY

– CHAPTER TWENTY-FOUR –

BACK TO THE FUTURE

'Are you okay?'

Matty looked over to the door as Lucy ran in and saw her eyes widen in surprise. He was helping his mum up from the floor. His dad stood by the bed where Morai had activated his own pod. The pod was at his feet and the tentacle-like vines writhed around him, but unlike what had happened with Ashna's damaged pod, these were not trying to pull people in.

'I'm fine,' said Matty, bringing his mum over to stand next to his dad. 'I'm really sorry, but I have to go.' He looked at his parents, grateful that, despite their fear and confusion, they had decided to trust him.

'What? Now?' asked Lucy. 'But there are poisonous flowers growing out there.'

'It is not poison,' said Morai in his matter-of-fact voice, as if nothing more strenuous than a tea party had just ended. 'In an endeavour to salvage this timeline, those flowers will wipe the memories of the soldiers in the house and those that have landed in the helicopter. I have also connected with the plants by the military vehicles. Flowers are growing there now.'

'But...' Lucy fumbled for words. 'But what about all these plants here? And the damage? Not to mention missing people?' She nodded at Matty's parents.

'The plants will wither and die as we leave. The prince and Ashna should never have been here, and the parents were meant to die, so their disappearance will restore balance. There is nothing I can do about the damage.'

'But there's still the fact that all the UNIT people are here and...'

'It is not a perfect solution,' admitted Morai. 'But it is the best I can do under the circumstances. Your help in saving the prince and defeating Ashna is appreciated.' He looked to Matty and his parents. 'But we must leave now.'

Matty's mum and dad each stepped in among the vines, next to Morai. Matty looked at Lucy with regret in his eyes. He would have liked nothing better than to have a proper goodbye. But there wasn't the time.

He wanted to tell Lucy just how much she had

come to mean to him over the few days since she had come into his life. She had helped him. Stood by him. Fought against Ashna with him. Had saved his life. But words seemed inadequate. So he smiled.

'Thank you.'

Then he joined his parents amongst the vines. He had to trust that this was the right thing to do. He was ready to return to the future; to his real life, whatever that might be. Yes, he felt scared and uncertain. But having his parents with him eased these feelings. Whatever his new life (old life?) held for him, he would deal with it, with their help. Light blazed and his surroundings started to fade. Lucy was waving, but then she seemed to be panicking about something. She was probably just upset that he was leaving. Sadly, there was nothing he could do about that. Everything was white now, and 1985 was gone.

The future began to coalesce before him. He felt hopeful.

LUCY

– CHAPTER TWENTY-FIVE –

HOME

As Matty stepped into the mass of vines, Lucy didn't really know what to say. He was leaving… forever. And so, presumably, she would be too. She knew that she'd never see him again. Although that made her sad, she was also looking forward to seeing Hobo. That's if he made it back OK. It now seemed like a long time since their adventure with Travers and Wells.

'Goodbye,' she whispered, smiling and lifting a hand to wave.

Movement in the corner of her eye suddenly caught her attention. There was a flower growing up out of the grass on the floor. *Oh no,* she thought, *Morai is trying to wipe my memory*. There was no way she was going to let that happen. She'd had quite enough amnesia to last a lifetime.

She spun to leave, only to find her way out of the bedroom blocked by more rapidly growing flowers.

She whipped her head from one direction to the other, but there were flowers growing everywhere. What could she do?

She held out her hand and stared at the ring, hoping that it would activate, willing it to take her home.

Pollen burst from the flowers, wafting through the air around her. She desperately held her breath, clutching a hand to her mouth and nose.

And then she felt it. The pull! The activation of the ring.

She was back in her room. Safe!

She took a deep breath, happy to be home. There was a funny smell. Floral.

'Oh no,' she whispered to herself, as she saw tiny particles floating around her room. The pollen had come with her. 'No, no, no, no, no. I can't lose my memories again.' She tried desperately not to inhale.

And now there were footsteps approaching. And a voice calling out. Her own voice... coming from just beyond her door.

'I'll be down in a minute!'

The time ring must have returned her to just before she had left. Lucy raced for the wardrobe, concealing herself among her clothes just as her earlier self entered the room. She heard the squeak of her bedsprings as the other Lucy sat down. She kept listening, trying to work out when exactly this was. She pushed the door a little, risking a peek. The other her was sitting on the end of her bed, an envelope in her hands. This was just before she had left.

The other her sniffed the air and gazed about. Lucy quickly pulled herself further into the wardrobe. And realisation hit her. The pollen! Her earlier self had breathed in some of the pollen that she had brought back. She had caused her own amnesia!

She blinked, her vision suddenly blurry. Her head felt funny.

The ring on her finger felt warm. It pulsed, almost as if it were alive.

She inhaled sharply.

Her head spun.

And once again she fell through the nothingness.

To be continued in Rampage of the Drop Bears *by Baz Greenland.*

George Ivanoff is an Australian author. He has written more than one hundred books for kids and teens, including the *Gamers* trilogy, *RFDS adventures,* the interactive *You Choose* series, the *OTHER WORLDS* series and the non-fiction *Survival Guides*; as well as a ton of educational books. He also recently wrote *Fear Frequency* for the Lethbridge-Stewart range of novels. George drinks too much coffee, eats too much chocolate and watches too much *Doctor Who*. (Only kidding… there's no such thing as too much *Doctor Who*.)

Check out his website for more info:
georgeivanoff.com.au

Other Lucy Wilson books in the series...

Avatars of the Intelligence by Sue Hampton

Curse of the Mirror Clowns by Chris Lynch

The Midnight People by John Peel

Christmas Crackers (short story collection)

The Bandril Invasion by Wink Taylor

The Brigadier & the Bledoe Cadets by Tim Gambrell

The Serpent's Tongue by Jonathan Macho

Attack of the Quarks by Chris Lynch and Tim Gambrell

The Phantoms of Tusker Rock by Christopher Bryant

Back in London by Sue Hampton and Tim Gambrell

The Keeper of Fang Rock by Andy Frankham-Allen & Tim Gambrell

The Children of January by Tim Gambrell

The Invisible Women by John Peel

Rampage of the Drop Bears by Baz Greenland

Lockdown (short story collection)